"We do
that any
from now on i

Lowering his voice, Mitch added, "Those kids in there are orphans because somebody purposely killed their parents."

Jill felt a shiver zing up her spine. Mitch was right. She grabbed his arm in a viselike grip. "You don't think the children are really in danger, do you?"

"I don't know." His eyes narrowed. "Are you willing to take the chance they aren't and let down your guard?"

"Of course not!" She didn't release her hold until she'd said, "I'm scared, Mitch."

To her chagrin, he replied, "Yeah. So am I."

The last thing Jill wanted to do was frighten the children more than they already were. Mitch seemed to sense her uneasiness. He paused and laid a hand of gentle comfort on her shoulder. "It'll be okay. I'll take care of everything. I promise."

VALERIE HANSEN

was thirty when she awoke to the presence of the Lord in her life and turned to Jesus. In the years that followed she worked with young children, both in church and secular environments. She also raised a family of her own and played foster mother to a wide assortment of furred and feathered critters.

Married to her high school sweetheart since age seventeen, she now lives in an old farmhouse she and her husband renovated with their own hands. She loves to hike the wooded hills behind the house and reflect on the marvelous turn her life has taken. Not only is she privileged to reside among the loving, accepting folks in the breathtakingly beautiful Ozark mountains of Arkansas, she also gets to share her personal faith by telling the stories of her heart for all of the Love Inspired lines.

Life doesn't get much better than that!

NIGHTWATCH

VALERIE HANSEN

Love Inspired

Recycling programs
for this product may
not exist in your area.

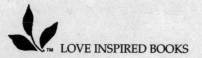 LOVE INSPIRED BOOKS

ISBN-13: 978-0-373-44460-1

NIGHTWATCH

www.LoveInspiredBooks.com

Printed in U.S.A.

Whoever receives one of these little children in my name receives me; and whoever receives me, receives not only me but Him who sent me.
—*Mark* 9:37

My husband and son were career firefighters
and my daughter also volunteered
before she went into nursing.

The men and women in the fire service
put their whole hearts into their work
and no amount of praise or thanks for their efforts
will ever be enough.

Thanks also to the dedicated CASA volunteers
who take over after disasters and help children
put their lives back together.

ONE

Boom!

Fire station windows rattled. Overhead lights vibrated. Captain Mitch Andrews froze, held his breath and braced himself with both palms on his desktop.

"*What* in the world was *that?*" someone shouted down the hallway.

Mitch figured every telephone in Serenity was already tied up by folks asking each other the same question. Their dispatcher would be fortunate to receive information giving a halfway accurate location of the problem, let alone a clear report of conditions at the scene.

A firefighter stuck his head through Mitch's office doorway. "What's going on?"

"I don't know. But it must be bad. Get ready to roll."

What he desperately wanted to do was grab a phone and call Jill; at least hear her sweet voice and make sure she was far from the current danger before he left the station. Duty didn't allow him that luxury. Not this time.

Sprinting for the hangar, he slammed his fist into the buttons that raised the bay doors. The siren mounted on the roof was starting to scream, rising and falling in pitch until he could barely hear his own voice over the wail.

"Jake, you round up the volunteers and get them moving as soon as you can," Mitch yelled, hailing the first man to clear the door. "I have a feeling we're going to need every piece of equipment we own on this one."

"Yes, sir," the engineer shouted. "What blew up?"

"Don't know yet."

Mitch listened to the details coming in over his handheld radio, then answered with, "Copy. All units responding to the vicinity of the county airport. ETA five minutes or less. Are ambulances started?"

The affirmative response gave him little comfort. Their small, local landing strip was located several miles outside town. If anyone had been in close proximity to an explosion violent enough to be felt this strongly at his fire station, they were going to need the coroner, not ambulances and EMTs.

Running, he grabbed his turnout coat, squashed his red captain's helmet over tousled, sandy-blond hair and jumped aboard the first engine out the door.

There was a bright, shimmering glow in the night sky as the driver headed west. Something had not simply blown up, it was also burning. Mitch gritted his teeth. There was only so much they could do to preserve life and property, no matter how state-of-the-art their equipment might be, and Serenity Fire Department was always struggling to keep up with new technology for both firefighting and medical aid calls.

"Was it a plane crash?" the driver shouted.

"Don't know." Mitch's heart was in his throat. "If it

was, I sure hope they missed the industrial buildings out that way."

"I wonder. Looks like a lot of fire for one small plane."

"Yeah," Mitch replied, releasing his breath in a whoosh. "It sure does."

Siren blaring, lights flashing, the engine slued around the last corner that brought them face to face with the conflagration.

Mitch's spirits sank like a stone in a bottomless lake. He could see the unscathed, white-enameled roof of the Pearson Products warehouse. However, part of the manufacturing building next to it was engulfed in flames and it looked as if that fire was about to spread to the attached, single-family dwelling—if it hadn't already breached the common wall.

Acting from years of training and experience, he shoved his personal dread aside and raised his radio. "Engine three on scene. One industrial building on fire. Other structures threatened."

As the first officer to arrive, Mitch was automatically in charge. "Engine two, follow me in. Engine one, lay a hose line and cover the rear."

"Engine two, copy."

"One copy."

"Chief," Mitch added, hoping and praying he'd get a quick answer, "are you responding?"

"Affirmative," Jim Longstreet replied. "I'm right behind you. ETA less than one."

"Be advised, we've got a rescue operation. Will you assume command?"

"Just pulling in now. I'll take over."

Tamping down the fear of what they might find if

they were already too late, Mitch broadcast, "Thanks. A family of five lives here. We'll lay a safety line and make access."

"They got *kids* in there?" the engineer beside him shouted above the howling of the engine's siren.

"Yes," Mitch replied. "Three."

Jill Kirkpatrick had formed the habit of monitoring local police and fire calls. It gave her more peace of mind when she knew what was going on in the country surrounding her isolated farmhouse, especially after dark.

Besides, she admitted to herself with a smile, she often listened in order to keep close tabs on Mitch Andrews. He was a very special person, the first and best friend she'd made in Serenity. They'd met when his fire department rescue squad had responded to the call for medical assistance after her husband's fatal accident, and Mitch had remained her anchor in the stormy days that had followed.

Being new in town and widowed so suddenly, Jill didn't know how she would have coped without his compassionate support and that of his fellow church members.

As she leaned closer to listen to the scanner, her long, blond hair swung against her cheeks and she tucked it behind her ears. She'd felt a strange shaking and heard a boom right before the radio had come alive. Something terrible must have happened. Not only was there a scary description being given of a fire, she could hear anxiety and dread coloring Mitch's voice as he broadcast to his crew. No matter how much he might deny it, he was definitely worried. Therefore, so was she.

Her initial response was to grab a jacket and her car keys and head for the door. Pausing, she almost changed her mind before peering out the window. Her blue eyes widened. The whole northern horizon was painted orange, yellow and red. Billowing clouds of smoke were lit from below as they formed a plume that blotted out the stars and rising moon.

One hand fluttered at her throat. "Oh, dear." That settled it. She had to go.

Quickly crossing the yard she climbed into her battered, well-loved red Jeep and started toward the glow in the sky.

Soon, acrid smoke was filtering in through the air vents. It carried pungent, unidentifiable odors that reminded her of melting plastic combined with household chemical cleaners.

"Lord, be with Mitch and whoever else is in danger," Jill prayed softly, fervently, her hands clenching the steering wheel. "Please, please, please."

She saw official vehicles converging at the far end of the one-runway airport so she pulled off the main road, parked where she wouldn't be in anyone's way, then proceeded on foot.

The closer she got, the worse the inferno looked. It had never occurred to her that any blaze could generate such a frightening roar. The noise reminded her of a crackling, pulsing jet engine and drowned out every other sound. Her eyes smarted. Her throat felt raw.

Knots of bystanders had gathered at the perimeter of the airfield. Men in yellow turnouts were busy shooting streams of water onto a house, apparently in an effort to save it from the encroaching flames.

Several of the closest casual observers were familiar to her from church so she greeted them with a somber look and a nod.

"Anybody seen Mitch Andrews tonight?" she asked, working to control her tone so no one would suspect how concerned she was. "I heard his voice on my scanner."

One of the elderly men hooked a thumb toward the burning home. "Yeah. He came outta there with two little kids, then handed 'em to the preacher's wife and went back inside."

Jill's heart leaped. Raced. Fluttered. There were children in that fiery death trap? And Mitch was in there rescuing them?

The urge to do something, anything, was so strong she nearly forgot herself and ran toward the fire. Only her respect for Mitch and his work kept her rooted to the more distant spot where she could safely observe.

Where *was* he? Could he be in trouble? Flames were licking up under the eaves in spite of the deluge from the hoses and it looked as if the entire house would soon burst into flames.

Jill's hands were fisted, her breathing shallow. "Come on, come on." It was barely a whisper, yet it carried the intensity of a shout, the passion of a prayer.

Suddenly, a familiar figure came hurrying out the front door. She instinctively knew it was Mitch in spite of the black-edged breathing mask covering his face and the shadows cast by the brim of his dripping helmet.

Arms laden, he raced off the porch, through the cascading waterfall from the fire hoses and out onto the sparse, wet grass. Using his body to shelter the child he was carrying he whipped off his mask while the rescued victim in his arms kicked, screamed and fought him.

Mitch looked up, made eye contact with Jill as if he'd sensed her presence and gestured frantically.

She whirled to check behind her, assuming he'd been signaling a fellow firefighter. There were none close by. Pointing to herself, she shouted, "Me?"

His nod was quick. His meaning clear.

She reached him in mere seconds. "What can I do to help?"

"Take him." Mitch's voice was a hoarse shout. If she hadn't noticed the moisture in the fireman's hazel eyes when he'd shoved a squirming, pajama-clad boy of about seven at her, she might have believed he was angry.

"Are there others? Should I wait?" Jill asked, holding tight to the thin, wriggling body of her new responsibility.

"No. I already gave Paul and Megan to Becky Malloy." He raised his radio. "Chief, we got all three kids out. No sign of the parents."

Jill waited until he was done speaking to ask, "What happened?"

"Don't know," Mitch said brusquely. "Just get Timmy out of here." His gaze softened and lingered on her face for mere moments, yet she could sense his special concern even before he said, "Take care of yourself, too, Jill. Watch your step. It's dangerous around here."

"I know. I'll be careful."

Seeing Mitch slip his mask and helmet on and turn, she blurted, "Wait! Where are you going?"

"Back inside. There are two more people to find."

"No!"

One look at the leaping, licking flames and she could hardly catch her breath. Mitch was going back into *that?*

Her first instinct was to grab his arm and hold tight to stop him, yet she knew that would be foolish. This was what he did, what he'd trained for. Interfering was very wrong, no matter how scared she was for his well-being.

"I have to. I'll be all right." His gaze rested for an instant on the child in her arms. "Just take good care of Timmy for me."

"I—I will."

As Mitch jogged away, Jill felt a burgeoning concern that left her weak in the knees. It wasn't only the firefighters she was worried about. She'd realized belatedly whose house this was. The Pearsons were members of Serenity Chapel as well as close friends of Mitch, so the adults he was still searching for must be the children's parents, Rob and Ellen. How hard this must be for poor Mitch—for all the local firefighters and police.

Her arms ached from holding on to the struggling boy, but she persevered. Right now, the most important thing was getting him away from the scene, keeping him safe and reuniting him with his younger siblings.

"Let me go!" the boy shouted. "Let me go."

"No. Sorry. I can't."

Jill knew there would be no reasoning with the child while he was so agitated. Keeping her replies calm and consistent was the best—the only—thing she could do.

It was trials such as this that her own childhood had prepared her for. That was why she'd volunteered as a foster parent in the first place, why she never said she was too busy or too financially strapped to take in another homeless, helpless waif.

It was her duty.

She'd trained for it by merely living the life she'd been handed.

Forced by the heat and flames to retreat or die, Mitch finally ordered his men to back off. Other teams had made access from the rear of the building so there was a chance one of them had successfully located the Pearsons. If not, there was nothing else anyone could do.

"Chief?" he radioed. "Any report on the adults from the house?"

"Negative. They thought they had one around back but it was just a nosy bystander getting too close."

"Copy."

As the fire continued to gobble up everything in its path, Mitch tried hard to keep from thinking about the people who might still be inside. There was nothing anyone could do for them at this point and he had a job to finish. A job he counted as a God-given assignment.

Suddenly, a wild-eyed woman in her thirties lurched toward him out of the haze and confusion. Her reddish hair was mussed, her short, white jacket sooty.

Under the circumstances, Mitch didn't pause to consider who she might be, he simply held out his arms to block her access to the disaster. "You can't go any closer, ma'am. It's too dangerous."

"Where is she?" the newcomer screeched, leaning to

peer past him at the ongoing destruction of the office and home. "Where's my sister?"

Mitch gritted his teeth. *Now* he understood. "You're Ellen's sister, Natalie, aren't you?"

"Of *course* I am. Get out of my way."

Ignoring the rolling of her eyes and her look of disdain, he shook his head slowly, sadly. "I'm sorry. We haven't been able to locate Ellen or Rob."

Instead of swooning or weeping as he'd expected, the woman began to scream, curse and pound him with her fists. "Well go find her! Don't just stand there, you idiot! Do something! Go back and look again!"

He did his best to fend off the blows without harming his attacker. A female sheriff's deputy noticed the one-sided altercation and quickly came to his rescue.

"This is the sister of the property owner," Mitch explained as the deputy restrained the panic-stricken woman. "Maybe she can wait in your car? Try to get control of herself?"

"Sure. No sweat. Sheriff Allgood's wife rode along with him. She can look after this lady for us."

Nodding, Mitch paused for only an instant before returning to the tasks at hand. His heart was heavy. He could certainly identify with the hysterical woman but he didn't dare give in to his personal feelings.

What he needed to do right now was concentrate on his job so he'd have less time to dwell on the loss of his friends. *Or on the fact that there were probably three new orphans in town*, he thought, clenching his teeth. How could a loving God have let any of this happen?

"Forgive me, Lord," he whispered as he gazed at the scene of destruction through stinging eyes. "And while

You're at it, help us all accept life without Rob and Ellen if they are truly gone. It's not going to be easy. Especially not for those kids."

TWO

Dozens of people continued to mill around the disaster scene, speaking mostly in whispers—awed, curious and yet horrified.

After wrapping Timmy in a gray blanket one of the bystanders had given her, Jill crouched, held the boy's hands, spoke softly and continued to try to comfort him. It seemed he either didn't hear her or had no intention of paying the slightest attention. Perhaps a little of both.

Pastor's wife, Becky Malloy, was perched on the open tailgate of a nearby pickup, cradling sleepy, eighteen-month-old Megan. Elderly Miss Violet Hanford, another member of both the fire department auxiliary and Serenity Chapel, rocked and soothed five-year-old Paul inside the cab of the same vehicle.

Timmy was most likely in shock rather than ill, Jill kept assuring herself. Nevertheless, as soon as one of the EMTs was available she intended to ask for professional advice.

In the meantime, there was nothing to do but keep an eye—and a hand—on him to make sure he didn't bolt. She figured she could have caught him if he'd tried to run under normal circumstances, but as emotionally overwrought as he was tonight, she wasn't sure he wouldn't be able to elude her if he wanted to.

Suddenly, his brown eyes widened. She felt his thin fingers tighten around hers. There was so much smoke in the air she wasn't sure if she was seeing tears of sorrow or if his eyes were watering because of the constant irritation.

She returned the squeeze and chanced a smile. "What is it, honey? Would you like to go sit in the truck with your brother? I'm sure it's much warmer in there."

Tim moved his head back and forth so rapidly his shaggy, uncombed brown hair swung like her little lapdog Mugsy's fur did when he shook himself after a bath.

Concerned, Jill leaned closer. "What's wrong? Tell me how I can help you."

Instead of answering, the boy tore his hand from hers and threw the coarse blanket off his shoulders. For an instant she was afraid he intended to flee. Then, he launched himself at her and wrapped both arms around her neck. The force of the unexpected tackle knocked her onto her back pockets in the dirt.

Timmy immediately scrambled aside, grabbed her wrist with both hands and tried to haul her to her feet. Although he wasn't speaking, she could hear whining, shuddery noises coming from deep in his small chest.

"It's okay," Jill said. "You didn't hurt me. I'm fine." She got up and began to dust off her jeans with her free hand. "See? No problem."

Still, the little boy wasn't pacified. Instead of continuing to face her, however, he ducked behind her legs.

That was what finally made her realize someone else was approaching. She recognized the puffy-eyed, disheveled woman as the one who had attacked Mitch earlier in the evening and braced herself to counter the same kind of irrational behavior.

It was the lost expression on the woman's tear-streaked face that softened Jill's attitude and caused her to offer proper condolences. "I'm so sorry. You're Natalie Stevens, aren't you? I'm Jill. We met in church. Your sister introduced us."

"What have they told you?" Natalie rasped. "They won't let me go closer to see for myself and they won't look for Ellen either. I've been all over the airport. Nobody's seen any sign of her."

"I don't think it's wise to discuss things like that in front of the children, do you?" Jill continued to soothe Timmy by slowly, gently stroking his hair.

"What? Oh. No, I suppose not." She began to pace and rub her hands together, never straying far before turning and repeating the tight circuit. "I can't understand what happened. Ellen almost never set foot in the office at all, and she certainly wouldn't think of working on a weekend. She can't have been in the office when it caught fire. She simply can't have."

"All I know is that they found the children in the main part of the house," Jill said. "The firemen got them out safely before that started burning, too."

Although the other woman didn't seem to be paying attention, Jill continued, "Don't you worry. We'll take good care of your niece and nephews until the proper authorities get here."

"Fine, fine." Natalie sent a distracted glance toward the pile of bent, scorched tin and ashes that had been the Pearson Products business office and began mumbling to herself as she wandered away. "Ellen can't be dead. I won't believe it. It's a mistake, that's all. A big mistake."

Timmy was still clinging to Jill's knees and trembling. She bent and wrapped him again for warmth before lifting and balancing his light weight on one hip.

Hugging her neck, he took a shuddering breath, buried his face in the folds of the blanket lying against her shoulder and began to weep.

Tears were a good sign, Jill realized, because that meant he was probably moving beyond his initial anger and shock. Instead of trying to get him to stop crying, she held him close and let him grieve, praying for the right words to eventually help soothe his pain and the wisdom to know when to speak.

She ached for this little one. For all of them. At times like this, when her heart was open and most empathetic, she was even better at relating to emotionally needy children.

Jill knew for a fact that Ellen Pearson had been a sweet person, a loving wife, a dedicated mother. Assuming everyone's sad assumptions were correct, Ellen had not meant to leave her dear ones. She had merely been caught in the wrong place at the wrong time.

Jill's own mother, however, had made a conscious choice. Mama had turned her back on her only child and had walked away—forever—without so much as a wave goodbye.

By the time several hours had passed, Mitch was mentally and physically exhausted. The engine crews had managed to preserve most of the factory and all of the separate warehouse but had lost the fight to save the home and business office. That was considered a good result under such difficult circumstances. As far as Mitch was concerned though, they had failed.

He'd grown close to the Pearsons when they'd moved to town a few years back and had started attending Serenity Chapel. He'd coached Timmy and Paul on the church T-ball team and had often envied the family's closeness.

Standing at the edge of the ruins, he was wiping his sweaty, gritty brow and remembering happier times when a hand clapped him firmly on the shoulder.

"We did all we could," Chief Longstreet said. "Even with the extra units from all over the county and everything we had in town, it was a tough fight."

"There's no chance Rob and Ellen managed to get out?" Mitch asked, unwilling to let himself believe his friends were really gone.

"Don't think so. Looks like the initial explosion blocked the office exit. If they were in there, they probably never knew what hit 'em."

"When we first got the call, I thought a plane had crashed. It's clear that didn't happen. So, did a gas leak start all this?"

"Could be. I've asked for investigators from Little Rock to come and look things over, just in case."

Shivers shot up Mitch's spine. "In case of what?"

Jim Longstreet gestured at the ground in the distance. "You've probably been too busy to notice but I spotted a few odd things. See the way some of the rubble is fanned way out from a central area? That doesn't look right to me."

"We all heard a blast."

The chief nodded. "True. And if this turns out to be an accident, I'll be happy to put that in my report. But until we can pin down a cause I'm going to keep needling the sheriff and anybody else who can give us some answers."

He concentrated on Mitch. "Look, I know these folks were good friends of yours. Why don't you go on back to the station and let the fresh crews finish mopping up? Things like this are tough enough when the victims are strangers."

"I can still do my job."

"I know you can. But we have plenty of extra help here now. I'll make it an order if I have to."

"I want to stay and see for myself first."

"Sorry. I'm not letting anybody except the coroner poke around in there until there's been an official investigation. Sheriff Allgood is gonna leave deputies to guard the site 24/7."

Mitch removed his helmet and raked his fingers through his damp hair. "This has to be accidental. Everybody loved Rob and his family."

The chief snorted. "I sure hope you're right."

Jill was waiting with Becky and the children when she saw a familiar figure approaching. She asked the pastor's wife to mind Timmy while she stepped away to speak privately with Mitch.

"I'm surprised you're still here," he said.

"We're waiting for someone from Children and Family Services to take custody of the kids." Reaching toward his hand, she stopped herself before they actually touched. "How are you doing?"

"I've been better."

"Any sign of other survivors?"

He shook his head slowly, sadly, his sober expression accentuated by the smudges of black ash on his face and the aura of loss that hung over him like a storm cloud.

"I'm so sorry. I talked to Natalie Stevens after she tried to beat up on you. She's a basket case."

Mitch huffed. "Yeah. A lot of us are."

He started coughing so Jill waited for him to quiet before she asked, "Why aren't you still working?"

"The chief is sending me back to the station early. It wasn't my idea. I just wanted to check that you were okay before I left."

How typical of him, she mused, touched by his concern. "I'm fine. I am looking forward to getting home and washing some of this smoke out of my hair, though." To her delight, that comment made Mitch chuckle cynically.

"Yeah. Right. Me, too," he said, raising his hand to swipe at the grime on his cheeks. "I guess I got a little dirty, huh?"

"A *little?*" Jill chanced a smile. "You look like an urchin and smell like a smoked ham."

"Thanks. You look nice, too, lady."

She sobered. "Sorry. I shouldn't have teased you like that. Not now."

"It's okay. Cops and firefighters have ways of coping that seem strange to civilians. So do E.R. doctors and nurses. We're always kidding around, even in really bad times. If we didn't, I don't know how we'd stay sane." He turned away as more coughing racked his body.

Jill took the chance he wouldn't mind and patted him lightly on the back. "Are you okay?"

"I will be. I always am." She saw him look past her

and zero in on the truck where Becky and the children waited. "Call me later and let me know how it goes with the kids, will you? I'll be at the station."

"Sure."

She yearned to give him a hug of consolation the way she had the boy but subdued the inappropriate urge. She and Mitch were merely good friends. He'd made his position clear at the outset of their relationship and she was in total agreement. She'd lost her mother at a young age and, just when she finally thought she'd gotten her life back on track, the love of her life had been killed in a freak accident. Twice was enough. Given Mitch's dedication to his dangerous profession, she was not about to open her heart to him and chance losing another loved one. As far as she was concerned, remaining alone was far better than risking a broken heart.

He bid her goodbye and walked away. Watching him go shouldn't have been so hard for Jill but it was. She knew what was wrong. She cared far more deeply for the valiant fireman than was wise.

Jill had greeted her exuberant little house dog, Mugsy, and was heading for the shower to try to wash the smell of smoke from her long, blond hair when her phone rang.

She almost let the answering machine take the call, then decided it might be important. "Hello?"

"You made it? You're okay?"

He didn't have to announce who he was. "Hi, Mitch. Yes, I'm fine."

"Why didn't you call me like you promised?"

"I was going to. I just walked in the door."

"Oh."

Sensing poignancy underlying his simple words her heart fell. "Did they find what you were afraid they would in the ashes?"

"We don't know anything for sure. Nobody does. Since neither Rob nor Ellen have surfaced, we have to assume the worst."

The sadness in his voice cut her to the quick. "I'm so sorry. I know you were close to the whole family."

"Yeah." She waited patiently while Mitch cleared his throat and prepared himself to go on. "I was just wondering about the kids. How are they doing?"

"Probably better than you and I are. Paul and Megan were sound asleep and Tim was only sniffling a little when the social worker finally showed up. She said she was going to take them straight to the county hospital to be checked out. I haven't heard anything more."

"Do you expect to?"

"Probably not tonight. I did put in a good word for myself, though. There's a chance they'll place the kids with me, at least temporarily, especially because I'm not fostering any other children right now."

"That's good news."

Jill knew he was deeply concerned so she tried to sound reassuring. "I'll stay in touch with the powers that be and make certain the kids are happy and well cared for no matter where they're sent. I promise." She smiled at the telephone as if it were Mitch's friendly face. "We should be celebrating the fact you saved all three of them, not fretting about a system that's only in place to *keep* them safe."

She chose not to elaborate about some of the less than ideal foster situations she'd found herself in while growing up. Mitch already had enough to worry about. She wasn't going to add to his burdens.

"How soon do you think we'll know?" he asked.

"I'm not sure. A lot depends on whether or not their parents had made prior arrangements with relatives or close friends in case of emergencies."

"You mean like choosing godparents?"

"Yes. Do you happen to know if they did?"

"Hmm. I don't think so. The kids were never very keen on their aunt Natalie and their uncle Thad hasn't been back in the States for very long, so I doubt they considered naming either of them as guardians." He huffed. "Young parents expect to live long enough to see their children raised."

"Yes, I suppose they do." Starting to think about her husband's untimely demise, she fell silent.

Sometimes it seemed as if that part of her past was little more than a dream; at other times pain pierced her all the way to her core. Lately, those uncomfortable moments had grown further and further apart and had hurt less. She supposed that was a good sign, although it meant that she was slowly forgetting the man she'd vowed to love and cherish for the rest of her days. That seemed wrong.

A softly spoken comment from Mitch brought her out of her reverie. Too bad she had no idea what he'd just said. "I beg your pardon?"

"I said take care of yourself. Get some rest."

"You, too," Jill told him. "You must be exhausted. It's been a rough night."

"I have had better. Thanks for taking over with Tim so I could go back to work. I didn't dare let go of him. He wanted to run back inside to look for his folks."

"I understand," Jill said, recalling memorable parts of the evening. "What do you know about Natalie Stevens?"

"Not much. Why?"

"Because, like I told you, she sure wasn't acting normal when I spoke with her."

"People get irrational under severe stress," Mitch said with conviction. "I've seen it happen over and over. They either deny that there's been a tragedy or try to place the blame on others. It's always tough. Especially when they show up on scene the way Natalie did."

"I'm so sorry she took her anger out on you."

"I have broad shoulders," he said, but Jill could tell the woman's unfair accusations had hit him hard. That, added to the fact that Mitch tended to blame himself whenever any task wasn't accomplished to his high standards, would weigh heavily on him for a long, long time.

"God's shoulders are even broader than yours," Jill said, trying to sound kind as well as wise. "Don't take too much on yourself."

"I have a job to do."

"I know. Since you keep telling me the Lord gave you that job, why can't you believe He also trusts you to do it well?"

There was nothing but silence on the line for what seemed like forever. Finally, Mitch simply said, "Night, Jill. I have to go," and hung up, leaving her staring at the receiver in disbelief.

She paused, then made a silly face. "Okay, mister, have it your way. Beat yourself up for every little thing, whether you really made a mistake or not. Be stubborn. See if I care."

She shook her head, disgusted mostly with herself. She *did* care. For Mitch, for the children, for the traumatized family, for the whole town. This tragedy would affect practically all of them in some way.

Yet it was Mitch's feelings that tugged the hardest at her heart. After all, he was a good friend and he faced danger often.

Picturing him as a victim instead of a rescuer, she suddenly experienced such a deep, personal sense of loss it made her literally ache.

The tears she had denied all evening returned and slid down her cheeks as she finally allowed herself to mourn for the lost—and for the survivors.

THREE

During a restless night, Jill had dreamed at least once of braving danger in order to save nameless, faceless children. By morning, she awoke feeling less rested than she had before the Pearson tragedy.

Coffee hadn't helped as much as she'd hoped it would, at least not so far. Refilling an enormous mug that had belonged to her husband, she took it with her and headed for the barn to begin her morning chores. There was nearly enough new spring grass to satisfy the few cattle she pastured but she still needed to be sure they had dry, baled hay to supplement their diet or they'd make themselves sick gorging on the fresh growth.

Shaggy, brown Mugsy danced along at her heels, his eagerness making her smile the way it always did. He was soon joined by her larger, black-and-white sheep-dogs, Salt and Pepper.

Spring was clearly on the horizon. Slim buds were poking skyward from amid the thick daffodil foliage at the base of the well house and the forsythia bush was starting to look as if its drooping branches had been sprinkled with bright yellow confetti. Jill smiled contentedly. That was one of the perks of living on the old farm. There were often surprises popping out of the ground or bursting into bloom to cheer her just when she needed a lift. Flowers even appeared in the lawn sometimes, as if God had strewn the seeds there to bring more beauty into her life and remind her she was loved.

She was just coming out of the barn, still accompanied by Mugsy as well as the ranch dogs, when the ringing of the cell phone in her pocket startled her. She fumbled and slopped coffee in her haste to answer.

"Hello?"

"Jill. It's me, Mitch."

"You sound upset. What's wrong?"

The moment he said, "They gave those poor kids to Natalie Stevens," Jill understood completely.

"No way. How did that happen?"

"I heard she showed up at the hospital and claimed them. I'm headed over there now to get some answers."

"Where? The hospital or Natalie's house?"

"The hospital. Some social worker named Brenda Connors is supposed to meet me there."

"I know her. She's the one I gave the kids to last night at the fire scene. I can't believe she'd allow someone to just take them away like that."

"Neither can I."

Clasping the little phone tightly, Jill didn't stop to censor her response. "Swing by here and pick me up on your way. I'm going with you."

"I was hoping you'd say that. I'll be there in ten minutes."

"Wait! That's too…" She was listening to dead air.

Making a face at the phone she began to jog toward the house. *Ten minutes?*

She wasn't prissy the way some women were but even *she* needed longer than that to get ready for a foray into the legal system surrounding the placement of homeless children.

"I can do this," Jill told herself firmly. "To help a nice guy like Mitch, I can do practically anything, including make myself presentable in less than ten minutes."

That statement made her smile. She wasn't preparing to help someone *like* Mitch, she was going to help *him*.

A part of her wanted to keep denying how special he had become to her while another part of her argued about how much his friendship and kindnesses had meant since Eric's accident.

She knew Mitch well enough to surmise that it was his sense of personal responsibility that had led him to pay so much attention to her. She didn't care what his motives had been. Not really. She just knew that she thanked the Lord daily that she'd met him, the same way she gave thanks for her Ozark home and the loving folks who had embraced her as part of their family and community when she'd been left all alone in a strange town.

Without a husband, Jill had wondered if she could make it in such rural surroundings. Yet whenever she'd had a need, there had always been someone ready to offer help. *Usually Mitch Andrews,* she added, although many other members of Serenity Chapel had also pitched in.

As she paused in front of her closet and reached for

a favorite, jacketed blue dress, she closed her eyes for a moment and whispered, "Thank You, Jesus," meaning every word from the deepest reaches of her heart. Her life might be nothing like she had imagined, but it was good.

Mitch's hands tightly gripped his truck's steering wheel as he drove. It wasn't Natalie's everyday reputation that worried him most, it was her erratic behavior at the fire scene. The woman had acted as if she could barely take care of herself, let alone look after three small children. The boys might be all right if she let them fend for themselves, but little Megan was far from self-sufficient.

He skidded to a dusty stop in front of Jill's white-painted farmhouse. She ran off the porch and climbed in the passenger side of his pickup before he had a chance to get out and open the door for her. Her blue eyes sparkled, her hair shimmered like gold and her face glowed as if she were embarking on an exciting adventure instead of preparing to enter a figurative lion's den.

"Thanks for coming with me," he said.

"Thanks for letting me. I worried about those kids all night."

"Yeah, me, too." Mitch drove off, staring at the road ahead as he delivered the bad news. "It's official. They found Rob and Ellen in the office."

"I'm so, so sorry."

When Jill reached across and briefly laid her hand over his, he tried not to flinch. "Thanks. They were special people."

"I never got to know them very well but I'm sure

they were." She smoothed the skirt of her dress, then folded her hands in her lap atop her clutch purse. "Is Brother Logan going to preach at their funeral?"

"Probably. It may be weeks before the crime scene techs and the coroner are finished and the bodies are released. That's another reason I was upset about Natalie getting the kids. There's no telling what an unstable person like her will do or say when she first hears the bad news, not to mention when we finally lay Rob and Ellen to rest."

"I totally agree. We need a judge's ruling about custody and we need it fast."

"How do we get that?"

"Probably through Ms. Connors. She'll request an immediate hearing and hopefully the court will also appoint a CASA volunteer to oversee the case."

"A what?"

"CASA. It stands for Court Appointed Special Advocate. Those people are trained to investigate everything and then speak for children who have been abused or neglected or who may be in danger. It can't be anybody like you or me who knows the family. It can't be a lawyer either. Or the police. This person has to be completely impartial. That's the beauty of the system."

Mitch doubted anyone could remain that unbiased, particularly when innocent children were involved. He knew he sure couldn't. "If you say so. Have you had experience with CASA before?"

"Yes," Jill said. "There aren't many volunteers out here in the boondocks but I do know of at least one. Samantha Rochard. She's a nurse at the county hospital."

"You trust her?"

"Completely."

Once again, Jill patted the back of his hand. Mitch managed a smile for her benefit. "Okay. If you vouch for her, that's good enough for me." His smile waned. "Hold it. What if she was one of the nurses who helped treat the kids last night?"

"I doubt that small connection would disqualify her," Jill said. "As a matter of fact, she's required to check with doctors and anyone else who may have had contact with the children before and after the fire, then make a written report to the judge."

"Meaning she'll realize how nuts Natalie is?"

"Let's pray that's the case."

"I think I'd better leave the praying to you," Mitch said. "Judging by what happened last night, the Lord isn't listening to me."

"I know exactly what you mean," Jill replied, surprising him with her candor. "After Eric died, it was a long time before I could really pray again. I just kept asking *why.*"

Mitch was about to apologize for not being able to save her injured husband's life when Jill added, "I imagine God was pretty sick of hearing me whimpering. It took me ages to realize I probably already had all the answers I was going to get."

He didn't know what to say. He shared her Christian faith, yet his own prayer life was nowhere near that satisfying. If he'd had more time to mull over her conclusion he might have commented. However, since they were pulling into the hospital's parking lot, he took that as a strong sign to keep his mouth shut.

He huffed quietly at that conclusion. Maybe—just maybe—he was getting more answers to his prayers than he'd thought, too.

* * *

Jill greeted middle-aged, graying Brenda Connors with a handshake and a smile, then introduced her to Mitch, purposely positioning herself to act as their go-between. It wasn't a comfortable place to be. Mitch was fighting to control his temper, which was totally understandable considering how close he was to the Pearson family. Jill simply wanted to keep the social worker on their side, at least until a trusted, sensible CASA member could be appointed.

"How soon before we can get a judge involved?" Jill asked Ms. Connors.

"I've already requested an emergency hearing. I'm picking up the children this afternoon. I've informed Ms. Stevens she had no right to take them the way she did."

"Why did the hospital staff let her?"

"Basically, she bullied them. A few of them knew she was the aunt so they assumed she had permission. Believe me, that kind of thing will *not* happen again."

She turned to Mitch, her eyes narrowing behind bi-focals trimmed in silver. "Is there definitive proof that the parents are both deceased?"

"Yes."

"Anything else you can tell me that might help?"

Jill interrupted. "Mr. Andrews was very close to the children and their parents. This is hard for him."

"I'm sorry," the social worker said. "But I need to know everything."

"Ask me whatever you like," he said flatly. "Those kids come first." He reached into his pocket and pulled out a cell phone. "Hang on a sec. I'll check with my chief and see if the investigation has turned up anything new."

As Jill watched and listened, she saw his hazel eyes widen, then darken as he began to frown. Her gaze darted to Ms. Connors and she noticed that the other woman was also paying close attention.

"I see," Mitch said. "Is that public knowledge yet?"

Jill found she was holding her breath.

"How about telling the kids' social worker? Can I do that without jeopardizing the case?" Mitch asked.

He apparently got the okay because he quickly bid the chief goodbye and faced Ms. Connors. Jill saw the muscles in his jaw clenching, twitching. Whatever he'd just learned, it was not good.

"The arson team from Little Rock found some chemical residue at the scene," he announced.

Jill assumed he meant plastic bits left over from the manufacture of the popular kitchen gadgets Pearson Products handled until he explained further.

"They're positive the office was bombed. That's what started the fire." Mitch's fists clenched at his sides. "This was no accident. Rob and Ellen were murdered."

Jill gasped. "Murdered? In Serenity? Things like that don't happen here. They just don't."

The social worker shook her head and nervously adjusted the position of her wire-rimmed glasses by pressing a finger to the bridge of her nose. "Apparently, it did this time. This changes everything. I'm not waiting. I'm going to pick up the children immediately."

"We'll come with you."

"That won't be necessary, Mr. Andrews. If I have problems I'll ask the sheriff for assistance."

"I wasn't talking about what Natalie may do," Mitch explained. "I was offering to help you calm the boys. They know me so well they even refer to me as their uncle most of the time. They've only seen you once and that was under terrible circumstances. You're about to take them from their aunt and she's liable to resist. Who do you think they'll listen to if things get rough, you or me?"

"All right." Brenda eyed Jill. "Are you free to accompany us? I carry the necessary infant seats and restraints for older children in my car but I may need help with the baby. She was really upset when I picked her up last night and I wasn't able to comfort her properly because I was driving."

"Of course. If you want, we can all go to my place to wait until you can get a temporary legal ruling."

"I wouldn't want to put you out."

"Nonsense. You know I'm already a foster parent so there should be no reason why my home wouldn't be okay, at least as long as you're there, too."

"And me," Mitch said firmly. "I'm not letting those kids out of my sight until I'm sure they're safe and well cared for. Rob would want it that way."

Although Jill nodded, she was still uneasy regarding what they were about to do. "Have you heard how hysterical Natalie Stevens was last night?" she asked Ms. Connors. "I worry about how she may react when you try to take the kids."

"I can handle her."

"Okay, if you say so. I really don't think they should spend time alone with her, at least not until she's seen a doctor."

"I agree. I've interviewed some of the hospital staff.

Their description of Ms. Stevens's behavior this morning was not comforting. If she hadn't sounded so calm and lucid when I phoned to tell her I was coming over later, I'd have called the police then and there."

"All right," Mitch said. "Let's stop standing around wasting time and get this show on the road. Jill and I'll follow you in my truck. Do you know how to get to Natalie's from here?"

"I have GPS. I'll find it. Just promise you'll both keep your distance when we arrive and let me do all the talking. It's what I'm trained for."

Jill heard Mitch mumbling to himself as he turned away. She couldn't make out every word but she was pretty sure he was either commenting on the job *he* was trained for or lamenting the loss of his friends.

She shuddered. *Murder. Here.* It was unbelievable. This was a nice, peaceful, little country town, not a big city where crime seemed to lurk in every alley and behind every locked door, and to ooze from the very cracks in the sidewalks.

Beginning to climb into Mitch's truck, she stopped in midmotion, one foot inside, one on the ground. An even more dire thought had just occurred to her. Whoever had placed that bomb and started the fatal fire was still out there somewhere. Loose. Dangerous. Perhaps planning another attack. And since there didn't seem to be any motive for harming Rob and Ellen, that meant their next victim might be just as sweet and innocent and well liked as they were.

"You all right?" Mitch asked, frowning and waiting for her to finish sliding into the passenger seat.

"No." Jill fastened her safety belt, then pulled the jacket of her dress closer and folded her arms to keep from shaking. "I can't help wondering who's going to be next."

"Don't borrow trouble. The fire last night was probably an isolated incident."

She eyed him across the seat, waiting 'til his gaze met hers before she asked, "Do you really believe that?"

It didn't surprise her one bit when he looked her in the eyes and answered bluntly, "No."

FOUR

The modest, red brick house Natalie Stevens occupied sat by itself at the far end of a cul-de-sac. The blinds were drawn and a folded newspaper lay at the base of the asphalt driveway. A few scraggly daffodils nodded in a narrow flower bed in front of the small, covered porch. Other than that, the place showed little landscaping and even less TLC.

Coming to a stop at the curb behind the social worker's car, Mitch looked at Jill. "Maybe she's not home."

"She has to be. Ms. Connors said she spoke with her. Remember?"

"That doesn't mean Natalie was here at the time. She could have been on a cell phone."

Growing more concerned by the second, he climbed out and circled the truck. By the time he reached Jill's door she was already standing there waiting for him.

He started to cup her elbow then thought better of it. He shoved his hands into his jacket pockets and simply fell into step behind her.

Brenda Connors was retrieving a briefcase from the trunk of her car. She straightened her short, fitted, wool coat as Jill and Mitch joined her. "Let me approach Ms.

Stevens first, one-on-one. But stay available. I'll signal if I need you."

"If Natalie attacks you, you'll need us for sure," Mitch said. "She was all over me like a crazy wild-cat last night at the fire. I wouldn't trust her as far as I could throw her. If she's hurt those kids, you may have to protect *her*." He felt Jill's calming touch through his sleeve.

"He doesn't really mean what he says," she told Ms. Connors. "It's been a long, trying twenty-four hours for all of us. I'm sure everyone will settle down as soon as we've determined where the children will be living, at least for now."

"Believe it or not, I do understand," the social worker replied. "I've been doing this job for a long time. There's not much I haven't seen or experienced." Pausing, she looked pointedly at Mitch. "Just keep re-minding yourself that the welfare and happiness of these three minors is our mutual goal. The smoother this transition goes, the better for the children."

Mitch gritted his teeth and nodded. She was right, of course. It was just that he hated feeling so helpless, so inadequate. He was a hands-on kind of guy. A person who liked to have all his ducks in a row. A man on a mission, if he were totally honest with himself. He felt at least partly responsible for Rob's and Ellen's deaths and he owed their children one hundred percent of his efforts.

Beside him, he sensed Jill's attention so he turned to her. There was tenderness in her expression mixed with something puzzling, something elusive, something compassionate to the point that he wondered if she'd just read his most private thoughts. There was a glimmer in her eyes that made them sparkle like flower petals sprinkled with drops of morning dew. Of all the previous times he'd seen her, had appreciated her loveliness, she had never looked more appealing.

"It'll work out, Mitch," she said. "In a few minutes we'll all be on our way to my farm and the kids will be able to relax. There's nothing like petting a dog to calm a person down. Mugsy's passed his socialization exams so he's a fully certified therapy dog. I can even take him on hospital visits with me if I want."

Mitch had to smile in spite of the tense circumstances. "Now *that* could get interesting. I can picture him tearing up and down hospital corridors at top speed and sliding the corners like a base runner trying to score on a double play."

To his delight, Jill mirrored his smile. "He's not quite that bad, you know. He may get a little too rambunctious at home but his manners are fine when I take him out."

"I'll believe that when I see it." Mitch rolled his eyes. "If that dust mop of a mutt wasn't always on the move, you wouldn't even be able to tell which end was which."

"You can tell right after I've trimmed the hair around his eyes. It grows back really fast though."

"Everything about Mugsy is fast," Mitch quipped. "Half the time he's just a passing blur."

"True. I wish I had his energy." Pausing, she sobered. "How are *you* doing today? You must have been up all night."

"Most of it," he replied. "I'll rest later. Right now I'm far too keyed up."

He began to watch the house more closely. Brenda Connors was standing at the open front door, apparently speaking with someone who remained inside. Since Brenda had not been invited to enter, he had to assume that her reception had not been a cordial one. That was no big surprise. When Natalie was behaving normally she wasn't very friendly. Under the present stressful conditions, Mitch doubted anyone was going to have much success reasoning with her.

Raised female voices carried to them. Mitch glanced at Jill, then back at the porch. His attention was diverted only momentarily, yet he almost missed seeing what happened next.

The screen door abruptly swung open. An arm shot out, palm forward. The thrust caught Brenda Connors in the upper chest area and shoved her backward so hard she staggered. For an instant he was afraid the middle-aged woman was going to topple off the porch.

Mitch began to run toward the house with Jill in pursuit. The door slammed with a noisy bang before he got there but he took the front steps two at a time just the same and confronted Ms. Connors while he steadied her. "What just happened?"

"She refused to admit me. I'm calling the police."

"The kids! Did you see the kids?"

"No."

"What about Natalie? How was she acting? Was she raving the way she did last night?"

The gray eyebrows arched and her eyes widened behind her bifocals as the social worker nodded. "I don't know what she was like when she attacked you, but she just scared the stuffing out of me."

Mitch didn't wait for further discussion. Wheeling, he almost collided with Jill as he left the porch and started to rapidly circle the modest, single-story dwelling. He'd never been to the house before and had no idea how he was going to get to those children. He only knew that he was going to do it. No matter what.

Jill didn't need any verbal clues to figure out what Mitch was up to. She'd known him long enough to be certain he was going to act, regardless of what Ms. Connors had said. In this instance she couldn't fault him, either. As a matter of fact, she intended to help.

Stepping past the frustrated, trembling older woman, Jill yanked open the screen, made a fist and began pounding on the hollow front door. The way she saw the situation, the more distraction she could provide, the better Mitch's chances were of reaching the Pearson children unobserved and spiriting them out of harm's way.

Was that legal? She doubted it. Nevertheless, she stood behind his actions with all her heart. There had been many times in her younger years when she had prayed for a champion, a knight in shining armor who would ride to her rescue as if she were a princess being held prisoner in a castle tower. Seeing Mitch playing that part for the sake of helpless little ones who were likely in danger of emotional, if not physical, abuse warmed her heart in ways she could hardly fathom.

"Open this door!" Jill shouted, continuing to bang on it. "Let us in this minute. Natalie? Do you hear me? I said open the door."

Behind her, Ms. Connors was covering one ear and practically shouting into her cell phone.

Jill made no effort to quiet her demands for the other woman's sake. On the contrary, she redoubled her assault.

Both her fists pounded until the wooden door rattled in its frame. "Open up! You have no right to keep us out. This lady is only doing her job."

Brenda grasped Jill's left arm. "Stop that. You're only making things worse."

"Leave me alone. I know what I'm doing."

"No. Stop. Wait for the police."

Once again Jill hammered relentlessly. "Did you hear that? The cops are coming," she yelled. "If you let us in before they get here you won't be in nearly as much trouble."

"Go away."

A-ha! Natalie was paying attention to her assault. The plan was working.

Since the unhinged woman was clearly standing right on the opposite side of the locked door, that probably meant she was not watching her nephews and niece closely. Therefore, Mitch had a much greater chance of success.

"We're not going away," Jill answered loudly. "You might as well let us in."

"No!" Natalie's reply was a little louder this time, raising Jill's spirits even more.

"Don't be ridiculous. You know you can't win. You can't bully us the way you did those poor people at the hospital. The police will make you open this door."

There was no immediate reply. Jill's heart began to pound so hard she could feel her pulse in her temples.

"Natalie?"

Still no answer came.

"Natalie Stevens," she screeched. "You get out here

and talk to me, you hear? I can help you. I will. I promise. Natalie? Natalie?" Her voice rose even higher and
she drew out the name. "Nat-a-lie!"

Trying the rear door, Mitch was thrilled to find that
it wasn't locked. He knew he was overstepping by going
into the house uninvited in the first place and wasn't
keen on adding forced entry to the charges he would
likely face.

Nevertheless, nothing was going to stop him. Not
at this point. The only thing that really mattered was
reaching Tim, Paul and Megan.

Hesitating, he heard Jill raising a ruckus at the front
of the house. Since she was not normally that outspoken
he had to assume she was doing it for his sake. Funny
how she seemed to understand so much without his
having to explain.

There were only two ways in and out of the kitchen
where he now stood—back the way he'd come or down
the hallway. Taking a chance that Natalie had at least
given the children a bedroom in which to sleep and
play, he headed down the deserted hall.

The first door he came to showed an unmade bed
and adult-size clothing scattered on the floor and chair
but no sign of the youngsters.

The door to the second room was closed.

Mitch eased it open.

Tim recognized him instantly and flew into his
arms. "Uncle Mitch!"

Paul followed his brother's lead while Megan remained asleep on one of the twin beds.

Holding tight to the sniffling boys, Mitch straightened, closed his eyes and choked back his own emotional reaction. "It's okay, guys. Don't worry. I've gotcha."

Tim took a shuddering breath. "Aunt—Aunt Natalie said we had to live with her now. She said…she said she was going to be our new mother."

Mitch's gut clenched. *How had she known they were orphaned?* He'd only heard the official confirmation himself an hour or so ago. He supposed she must have assumed the worst, given the destruction from the fire and all, but there was still no excuse for breaking it to the boys as bluntly as she had.

"Nothing is settled," Mitch said, giving the children a hug before lowering them to the floor. "Right now, we need to go. Do either of you have shoes?"

"Uh-uh. We got these dumb clothes at the hospital. I want my superhero shirt."

With his lower lip trembling, Paul agreed with his big brother. "Yeah. Me, too."

"Sorry, guys. First things first."

Mitch quickly approached the sleeping toddler and folded a blanket around her. Megan barely stirred as he picked her up. "Okay, boys, time to go. Be quiet now, you hear? We're going to leave by the back door."

"We're sneaking out?" Timmy whispered, his reddened eyes widening as he swiped the back of his wrist across his upper lip and sniffled noisily. "Way cool."

"Yeah, cool," Paul echoed.

"Not if your aunt catches us. Be very quiet."

Mitch halted at the bedroom doorway and looked toward the kitchen. So far, so good.

He also listened intently, fully expecting to hear Jill

and Natalie shouting at each other as they had been moments before.

The silence was so unexpected it made him shiver. That was definitely not a good sign. If Jill wasn't hollering that meant she'd either been stopped or had, for some reason, decided it was unnecessary to continue.

Either way he was in a pickle. If Natalie was no longer guarding the front door, where was she?

Jill began to tiptoe through the dry, patchy grass, peering in the side windows as she came around the house. There wasn't much opportunity to see in except where the blinds left slight gaps at the edges of the window frames. If she hadn't known otherwise she would have thought the house was deserted.

She turned the final corner and spied a small, square rear porch. There were only two steps to climb and she did so very cautiously. Her hand was on the knob, ready to open the door, when she heard a primal scream that reminded her of a nature show about African lions that she'd recently watched on TV. Shivers zigzagged up her spine and lifted the fine hairs at the nape of her neck.

Easing the door open a crack she peeked inside. Her breath caught. She covered her mouth with her free hand to keep from gasping aloud at the scene before her.

Natalie Stevens was standing with her back to the exterior door—and to Jill—facing Mitch and the three children he'd come to rescue. They were clustered in another doorway, apparently about to try to make their escape, and Natalie stood between them and freedom.

Lifting her index finger and laying it across her lips, Jill signaled Mitch. With an almost imperceptible nod he acknowledged her. She could tell his mind was racing, trying to decide what to do next, and she'd have felt a lot better about it if he hadn't looked as though he was furious—with *her*.

Well, too bad. Jill wasn't particularly eager to face the other woman's irrational anger either, but she saw no options. Unless someone distracted Natalie and got her out of the way, Mitch and the children wouldn't be able to safely pass. If he truly was mad at her for helping, they'd settle that later.

Jill knew Mitch would have simply pushed his way out if he had been alone. While carrying and guarding the children, however, his hands were literally full. He'd never do anything to endanger them. And the way Natalie was cursing and wildly waving her arms, it looked as if they were running out of time. If someone didn't act soon, Mitch would find himself—and the children—in the midst of a melee.

Jill was still trying to decide what to do when she gave the door a gentle push. It not only opened, it squeaked!

Natalie stopped midtirade. Whirled. Gaped at Jill. Then her jaw snapped closed and her eyes narrowed. "You! Out of my house. Get out of my house!"

That was Mitch's cue. With the boys in tow, he bent low over Megan to protect her and made a dash for the door.

Although Jill stepped aside, he jostled her in passing.

She recovered her balance, slammed the door behind the last child and followed Mitch's gruff order to "Come on."

They reached the front lawn just as Sheriff Harlan Allgood rolled up, red and blue lights flashing.

Mitch made straight for the police car and stopped on the opposite side of it. By this time Megan was not only fully awake, she was bawling in fright.

With open arms, Jill beckoned to Mitch. "Give her to me."

Although his expression showed reluctance, he did hand over the squalling toddler. Jill watched him ignore the sheriff long enough to crouch and comfort the frightened little boys.

"It'll be okay, guys. I'll do my best to make sure your aunt doesn't take you away again," Mitch said. "I promise."

Then he straightened and faced the lawman. "Hi, Harlan. I just went inside and got these kids. And I'd do it again if I had to. I don't care if Natalie Stevens is their kin, she had no business taking them out of the hospital without permission." He gestured toward the social worker who was rapidly approaching. "Ask her. She'll tell you they don't belong in that house."

Just then, a dusty, battered pickup truck slued around the corner and sped recklessly toward the gathering in front of Natalie's house.

Jill didn't recognize the driver. "Who's that?"

"Thad Pearson," Mitch replied, his scowl deepening. "Looks like he got word through the grapevine. Just what we need. Another relative to argue with."

"He's Rob's brother, right? I'd never actually met him but I had heard there was a strong family resemblance."

"Thad and Rob do—did—look alike. That's about all they had in common. Thad's always been the fighter, which undoubtedly helped him when he was a Marine."

He gave Jill a look of disdain. "See that you stay out of it this time. I mean it."

"Hey, you didn't seem to mind my intervention a few minutes ago."

"Yeah, well, this is different. Thad's nobody to mess with. His temperament is not what I'd call an asset."

Neither is yours if you keep getting upset with me for trying to help, Jill thought.

Mitch stood his ground, apparently braced to defend the children, as Thad jumped out of his truck and jogged closer, fists clenched, posture rigid. Jill could tell how angry the man obviously was. That observation didn't do a thing to help calm her already taut nerves.

Before the newest arrival could reach the children, Harlan stepped between him and the others with his hands raised. "Simmer down, son. I've got everything under control."

As Jill watched Thad's face and posture she could see his inner struggle. Finally, he nodded and stopped acting so aggressive. At least she thought he did. Given the volatility of the whole confrontation and all the parties involved, it was hard to tell. Personally, she wished she were locked inside the sheriff's car with the children while these stupid men settled their disagreements.

Harlan eyed them as a group. "Okay. All you people wait right here and behave yourselves. Nobody's going anywhere till we get this mess sorted out. Y'hear?"

Mitch nodded and so did Thad. Jill was rocking and comforting the littlest Pearson as she answered, "We wouldn't dream of leaving. Believe me, we're *very* glad to see you."

In the background she thought she heard Thad muttering curses, although nothing he said could have equaled the vitriol in Natalie's recent tirade.

Given a choice, Jill decided she would much rather have to face down any or all of these angry men than spend one more minute with that hysterical, bad-tempered woman.

FIVE

Considering how long Mitch had figured he'd probably have to cool his heels in jail for taking matters into his own hands, the entire morning had ended surprisingly well.

Natalie had been given a sedative by the EMTs Harlan had summoned. Thad had settled down on his own once he'd realized that his sister-in-law was not going to be given custody of the children.

Brenda Connors had not only convinced the police that Mitch was one of the good guys, she'd managed to get a judge to hear the Pearson case in chambers.

"All right," the elderly judge had said. "If you have no objections, Ms. Connors, I'm going to appoint Samantha Rochard to represent the Pearson children."

Mitch had been holding his breath until the social worker had answered, "Fine with me, Your Honor."

"And as for temporary custody, I see you recommend they be placed with Jill Kirkpatrick. Is that correct?"

"Yes, Your Honor." Brenda had smiled at Jill where she and Mitch stood aside tending the three orphans.

"Done," the judge had said. "And I wish you all the best. I'll have my clerk draw up the official papers."

Beside him, Mitch had heard Jill whisper, "Thank You, Lord," while the social worker thanked the judge and shook his hand.

That settled, they were all on their way to Jill's. Mitch followed in his truck because Jill and the children had to ride with Ms. Connors to keep everything legal.

As soon as Tim climbed out of the car, he made a beeline for Mitch and grabbed his hand, tugging him along. "Are we gonna go home pretty soon, Uncle Mitch?"

He had to answer truthfully for the child's sake. "No, son. I'm sorry. But you'll like staying with Miss Jill. She has lots of animals here for you to see and play with."

"I want my mama," Paul whimpered, sidling up to his brother and scuffing his bare toes in the dust.

Tim pulled Mitch closer and cupped a hand around his mouth before he said, "He doesn't get it, but I do. Mama and Daddy are in Heaven. Right?"

"That's right." Mitch was doing his best to keep from showing the depth of his emotions. He knew from his experience on the fire department, and with church youth, that kids who had been raised going to Sunday school simply accepted the loss of a loved one because they'd been taught about eternal life. He'd often wished he could have that kind of childish, unquestioning faith.

"I'm gonna miss my daddy," Tim said.

"I know you are. But don't worry about that right now. First we need to get you and your brother and sister settled here. Then maybe we'll go into town and buy you all some new clothes."

Tim brightened. "Yeah! Miss Jill says she might have

some stuff for Megan to wear but not so much for Paul and me. We're big boys."

"I know you are. You're growing like a weed."

Sobering, the seven-year-old nodded. "Uh-huh. That's what my dad always says." He tightened his grip on Mitch's fingers and Paul grasped his brother's hand as they all headed for the house.

The little boy's firm grip made Mitch feel so parental he was astonished. If this was any indication of how it felt to be a father, he doubted he was up to it. That child trusted him to make everything right again, to fix what was broken in his young life and set him on the right path. What an awesome responsibility.

Carrying Megan, Jill ushered everyone inside, to the obvious delight of Mugsy. He wiggled and danced and tried to lick the boys' faces in greeting.

"Mugsy," Jill commanded, making a hand motion at the same time. "Down. Behave yourself."

Mitch had to chuckle at the poor, rapidly panting little dog's Herculean efforts at self-control. He could sure identify. He'd felt the same unbelievable urge to move, to act, when he'd seen Natalie physically rebuff Ms. Connors, not to mention when Jill had foolishly tried to intervene. And things had gone from bad to worse when Thad Pearson had arrived, acting as if he intended to take the house apart, brick by brick, to get to the kids.

Giving credit where credit was due, Mugsy was doing a better job of holding his feelings in check than Mitch—or Thad—had.

"Megan and I are going to go make everybody something to eat," Jill said. "Who else wants to help?"

The only one who jumped up and dashed to her side

was Mugsy. "Okay. I have one volunteer." She was grinning at the boys. "How about you two?"

Tim cast a questioning glance at Mitch, saw him nod and dutifully responded, taking Paul's hand and urging him to do the same.

As soon as he was alone with the social worker, Mitch asked, "How long will they be allowed to stay here?"

"That's hard to say. Since there was a crime involved, they may eventually be moved into protective custody while law enforcement sorts it all out. For the present, let's just take one day at a time," Ms. Connors said.

"Okay." Frustrated, Mitch folded his arms across his chest and shook his head slowly, contemplatively. "I guess that will have to do. I just wish…"

"I know." She gave him a motherly pat on the shoulder. "You care. We all do. Here's my card. If you learn anything else that may help, please let me know ASAP."

"Will do." Slipping the business card into his pocket, he suggested, "What about asking the sheriff to keep a special eye on this place?"

"Done," Ms. Connors said. "They'll be in contact with Jill and let her know what they're doing. She'll have to notify Harlan's office whenever she plans to leave the farm or may be temporarily out of touch. I've already suggested that she carry her cell phone with her at all times, just in case."

The ominous mood of that warning gave Mitch the shivers. "You think the kids may be in danger?"

"Probably not. However, I prefer to cover all the angles rather than be caught unaware." She eyed him quizzically. "Do you happen to live close?"

"No, but I can arrange to stop by on my days off. I'd planned to, for the kids' sake, of course."

"Of course. Perfectly understandable."

Although there was no inference of improper behavior in the woman's words or her tone, Mitch nevertheless felt his cheeks warming. He and Ms. Connors both knew that the children were not the only reason for his planned diligence. He wanted to watch over Jill, too. He had ever since he'd first met her.

In the kitchen, Jill put little Megan in a high chair so she could take off her own jacket. She gave the toddler crackers to munch to keep her occupied.

Then she donned an apron and taught the boys where she kept the bread, lunch meat and condiments while she prepared a pot of macaroni and cheese.

"You two will be a big help around here, I can tell," she said, smiling. "We have a couple of important rules, though. One, no touching the stove. *Ever.* And two, please ask before you try to fix yourselves something to eat unless I'm watching. It's my job to see that you don't get hurt, okay?"

Two simultaneous nods satisfied her. All children forgot rules, of course, but this much cooperation was definitely a good start. They were good kids. She could tell. Megan might get into things once she was turned loose to explore but Jill had long ago childproofed her home so even a curious toddler was safe.

Plus, she had Mugsy and the ranch dogs to keep her wards entertained. Mugsy was wiggly but very gentle and the larger dogs, being bred to herd, would naturally try to keep the kids together like a flock of sheep whenever they were outside.

Her smile widened then became more reserved as Mitch joined them in the kitchen. If he was still upset with her she didn't want to make more waves.

"Ms. Connors had to leave. Mind if I stay for lunch?" he asked, acting suitably penitent.

Jill was satisfied that he'd gotten over his earlier annoyance, at least enough to make him good company. "Not at all. The boys have been helping me set the table. Would you mind lifting down some plates for them? That cupboard is too high."

"I know."

"Yes, I suppose you do. You've eaten here often enough."

"Not *that* often."

It tickled her to see the blush on his cheeks. "Okay. Maybe not that often. But you do know where everything is kept. Just watch that Paul doesn't slip another slice of bologna to the dog. I saw him do it once already."

Her gaze darted briefly to the younger boy and she smiled benevolently at his contrite expression. "I understand. Mugsy can be an awful pest when he wants a treat. Just ask me the next time you want to feed him. All right?"

Paul mumbled, "Uh-huh," while his brother nudged him in the shoulder and warned, "We gotta be real good or we'll get sent back to Aunt Natalie."

Instead of being helpful, that brought tears to Paul's brown eyes. When Mitch knelt in front of the unhappy boy and began to quietly speak to him, Jill's heart clenched. She had to bite her lip to keep from weeping at the tender sight. Here was a big, strong man stooping to comfort a child who was not even his own.

Touched to the depths of her soul, she averted her face until she could regain better control of her emotions. This was what the perfect family of her dreams looked like. And, although she had long ago given up the notion that she could have this kind of life on a permanent basis, she gave thanks that she was being granted the blessing of partaking in something so close to it.

A chorus of gruff barking from the outside dogs jarred her back to reality. Her eyes met Mitch's as he straightened. "This is almost done cooking and I can't leave it," she told him. "Will you check on the dogs, please? They don't usually bark like that."

"Sure. Maybe they've spotted a skunk. That would liven up this party."

"Don't even joke about something like that. Not unless you plan to stay and help me wash the smell off them if you're right."

He arched an eyebrow. "Gotcha. I'll be right back." Pausing, he looked at Tim and Paul. "Y'all be good while I'm gone."

"Yes, sir," Tim piped up as he grabbed his brother's hand. "We will."

Jill was grinning foolishly but she didn't even try to subdue her amusement. Here they were, five individuals thrust together by disaster, yet they already sounded like a normal family. Of all the children she'd cared for, these were the first who seemed this much like her own.

That's because Mitch is here, too, she told herself, slightly abashed by the obvious truth. Mitch was what completed the pseudofamily. Too bad his reasons for being there were because of the children for whom he felt such strong accountability.

She was positive that was why he'd always paid so much attention to her, too. He was the kind of guy who took on far more responsibility for the results of his harrowing profession than was warranted. He was there because he blamed himself for not only the deaths of Rob and Ellen Pearson, but also for not being able to save her darling Eric.

Forcing herself to concentrate on the boiling pasta in the pan, she had almost managed to bring her wandering thoughts under control when she heard Mitch shout.

She froze, listening, trying to hear what he was saying beyond the closed door and windows.

Tim left his brother and sister and clambered up on a chair next to the dining table. From there he could see into the yard. He pressed his little nose against the glass, then turned to Jill in wide-eyed wonder, his jaw gaping.

"What is it, honey? What do you see?"

"Uncle Mitch is wrestling. And some mean dogs are trying to bite him!"

"That can't be. I don't have any mean dogs."

Jill took the hot saucepan to the sink and set it where it wouldn't accidentally be upset, glanced out the window, then immediately grabbed the largest iron skillet she owned.

"Stay right here and mind Mugsy," she ordered. "You can keep watching from the window if you want but don't you dare set foot outside. Got that?"

Without waiting for an answer she jerked open the back door and braced herself for battle, the heavy pan brandished like a real weapon.

The moment her herding dogs heard her whistle and

saw she was nearby they abandoned their task of worrying their grounded quarry and galloped toward her, tails wagging.

Once they were out of the way she could see that Mitch lay prostrate in the dirt in front of the barn. There was no one else in sight.

She cast the pan aside and ran to him, falling to her knees at his side. There appeared to be traces of blood and dirt in his hair but he seemed otherwise unhurt.

He moaned and opened his eyes, then immediately tried to sit up.

Jill restrained him by placing her hands on his shoulders while he gingerly probed the back of his head with one hand.

Because he was looking around so rapidly and was obviously confused, she said, "Take it easy. Everything's fine. I called off the dogs. How did they get you down, anyway? Did you trip?"

"No!" It was guttural bark. "What are you doing out here? I told you to stay in the house."

"Helping *you*." She made a face at him. "And you're quite welcome."

He was struggling to stand so Jill assisted.

"Where is he? Is he gone? Did you see which way he went?"

"Who?"

"The prowler," Mitch said, swaying with the effort of maintaining his balance. "I didn't just fall down. I was grabbed and hit from behind. Somebody was hiding in the barn."

"Who was it?"

"I don't know. I didn't get a good look at him. He was wearing a mask."

So that's what Timmy had meant when he'd said Mitch was wrestling. The hair at the nape of her neck prickled. She tensed, instantly alert, and wished she hadn't dropped her makeshift weapon.

"I—I didn't see anybody running off when I came out, but maybe the boys did. They were watching from the kitchen."

"Then let's go ask them," Mitch said, starting to lead the way with an obviously increasing ability to stay on his feet. "Then I want to call the sheriff and have him go over this place with a fine-tooth comb. I aim to find out what some lowlife was doing messing around your barn."

"Maybe it was just a thief," she offered.

He reached the back door and paused with his hand on the knob before opening it. "Look. We don't dare assume that anything that happens from now on is innocent or simple." Lowering his voice he added, "Those kids in there are orphans because somebody purposely killed their parents. Remember that the next time you decide to leave them alone and rush headlong into a situation you're not prepared for."

Jill felt a shiver zing up her spine and tingle every nerve in her body. Mitch was right. She was the caretaker of all that was left of Ellen and Rob's family. The importance of that responsibility was mind-boggling.

She grabbed Mitch's arm in a viselike grip. "You don't think the children are really in danger, do you?"

"I don't know." His eyes narrowed. "Are you willing to take the chance they aren't and let down your guard?"

"Of course not!"

"Then come on. You phone Harlan while I talk to the boys and see if they saw more than we did."

She didn't release her hold until she'd said, "I'm scared, Mitch."

To her chagrin, he replied, "Yeah. So am I."

Mitch managed to get the kids calmed down enough to sit still at the kitchen table and Jill was able to rescue most of the mac and cheese.

She hadn't wanted to eat at all but Mitch had insisted they must keep up a calm front for the sake of the children and she had to agree.

They were halfway through the meal when Sheriff Allgood pulled quietly into the yard. The two dogs that had spotted the prowler also greeted the patrol car and loudly announced its arrival.

Mitch crumpled his paper napkin and rose from the table. He looked pointedly at Jill. "Stay here and finish lunch. I'll go fill him in on what happened."

She desperately wanted to ask him to stay, to continue to keep them all company, but she didn't dare. The last thing she wanted to do was frighten the children more than they already were. Between being snatched by their hysterical aunt and then seeing Mitch fighting a masked nemesis, they'd already had plenty of unwanted excitement for one day. So had she.

Mitch seemed to sense her uneasiness. He paused and laid a hand of gentle comfort on her shoulder as he passed her chair. "It'll be okay. I'll take care of everything. I promise."

She nodded without comment. That was just like Mitch. He truly believed everything was up to him, the same way he thought that success or failure on a cosmic scale was in his power.

She knew better. She'd seen how it had hurt him when he wasn't able to accomplish everything he set out to do and she'd often prayed that God would help him see the truth. Try as he might—as any of them might—there were some things in the universe that were not within their sphere of influence. Death was one of those terrible events that defied human understanding. It seemed so random, so unfair, yet her pastor taught that God was sovereign. And loving.

Jill felt a tear slide down her cheek and surreptitiously brushed it away so the children wouldn't notice. There were times, like now, when she struggled to accept what had transpired. Good people had been murdered. Children had been orphaned. And Mitch…

A tiny hand began to pat her arm. It was Megan. The lovely, doe-eyed, curly-haired child had sensed her unhappiness and was offering solace. As Jill had often noted in the past, her heavenly Father had sent someone to let her know she was His child and that she was loved.

Rising, Jill lifted the little girl in her arms, carried her to the sink and rinsed the sticky orange cheese off her cheeks and her hands.

"Okay, gang," she said with forced lightheartedness, "Shall we go see what Uncle Mitch and the sheriff are up to? We can't let them have all the fun with Salt and Pepper."

Tim frowned. "With what?"

"Salt and Pepper. Those are the names of the dogs outside that jumped on Mitch," Jill explained. "They don't usually play so rough. I'll tell them to be very careful and not knock you boys down."

"I ain't scared," Tim insisted, puffing out his thin chest. "I can take care of my brother and sister, too. I'm seven."

"I know you are. And I already appreciate how much you've helped me." It thrilled her to see Tim beaming with pride. He was truly a "little man" in a child's body, as were many firstborn or only children. They took charge and fulfilled adult expectations as well as they possibly could. It was their nature.

It was *her* nature, too. Nobody survived abandonment and one foster home after another without becoming extremely self-reliant. For as long as she could remember she had felt as if she were standing alone against the whole world. And sometimes, like the day Eric had died, she'd felt that even God had forsaken her.

That wasn't true, of course. She knew in her deepest heart that God loved her. And now it was her duty to show that divine love to others; to demonstrate the same kind of unconditional acceptance and support that had brought her through all kinds of trials.

Opening the back door and seeing the sheriff's car made her shiver. There was little doubt that this current ordeal was far from over. She knew it and Mitch knew it. They didn't have to discuss everything for her to be certain. She could read him like a beloved book and she strongly suspected that he could read her, too. That wasn't all bad. It meant that whatever tests came, they would instinctively be able to face them together and triumph, just as they had when they'd rescued the children from their aunt—even though Mitch didn't approve of her taking so much incentive.

Would what lay ahead be even half as bad as what had already happened? Jill hoped and prayed that was not so. Because if it was, she and Mitch—and especially the innocents the good Lord had placed in her care—would be in terrible danger.

SIX

Mitch tensed when he saw Jill and the children approaching. The farm dogs were circling them in greeting while Mugsy did his best to keep from being stepped on by man or beast. Having those animals sticking so close was good. It meant they'd provide at least some protection; although the dumb dogs had jumped on *him* when he went down instead of chasing the guy who had decked him.

The sheriff extended his hand and shook with Mitch to complete their exchange of information. "All right. If you remember any other details give me a holler. In the meantime, keep everybody out of the barn. I want to check it carefully before I leave. Even if I don't find any clues we'll increase our patrols out this way. You sure you didn't hear any vehicles after you were knocked down?"

"I was pretty out of it," Mitch admitted, chagrined. He motioned to Jill and her little group. "Did any of you hear anything funny?"

"I honestly wasn't paying attention," Jill said. "I was too worried about you."

"Thanks." He knew his cheeks were getting rosy because he could feel the increasing warmth. "Tim said he thought he saw another man besides the one who jumped me. Right, buddy?"

The seven-year-old ducked his head. That shy response puzzled Mitch. Tim had sounded positive when they'd talked about it before, yet now he was barely acknowledging their conversation. In addition, he had taken up a defensive position behind Jill and had pulled his little brother with him. For kids who had chattered all during their hurried lunch, they were sure acting strange all of a sudden.

Maybe it was a negative reaction to the police car, although Mitch could think of no reason for them to be afraid of Harlan. The bear of a man could be a little boisterous sometimes but he was also built a lot like a beardless, department-store Santa Claus. His persona was anything but threatening. Most children took to the sheriff immediately. Of course, considering the traumatic events of the past few days, Mitch supposed it was a wonder these poor kids were coping as well as they were.

Cradled in Jill's embrace, Megan was sucking her thumb and fighting sleep. Seeing the toddler with one little arm wrapped partway around Jill's neck and her tousled head lying on Jill's shoulder, Mitch suddenly felt so protective it floored him.

While Harlan checked the barn, Mitch joined her and the children. "Looks like one of us has conked out."

"Uh-huh. I'm not surprised. I was planning to bathe her before I put her down for a nap but I think I'll just wait 'til tonight. She needs sleep more than she needs fussing over. As soon as she's rested I want to take her and the boys into town and buy them a few things. They especially need shoes."

"I can take them," Mitch offered.

"Sorry. Not legally you can't. Now that they've been placed with me, the only people who can take them anywhere without me—or even babysit—are folks who've been court approved or are official foster parents, too."

Falling into step beside her as she headed back toward the house, he asked, "How hard is that to do? I mean, suppose I took the class or whatever else is required? Would I be able to help you out with them after that?"

She shrugged. "I can't see why not. I know that statistically there are never enough homes available for all the families in need. If you have Ms. Connors's number, why not give her a call and ask about it?"

"Good idea."

Mitch held the door for all to pass except the pair of farm dogs. He stepped into the doorway to block their entrance, pointed to the barn and commanded, "No. Go bother Harlan."

To his surprise and amusement they loped off as if they understood exactly what he wanted and were more than happy to obey. What would Jill think of that? he wondered. She was already teasing him about knowing where stuff was kept in the kitchen. Having her dogs listen to his orders would probably cause her to raise an eyebrow, that's for sure. Too bad he didn't have the same effect on her that he did on her pets. Lately, it seemed as if the more sensible advice he gave, the more likely she was to contradict or ignore it.

Chuckling wryly, Mitch wandered through the kitchen and lingered in the living room, waiting for Jill to return from putting Megan down for her nap.

Tim and Paul had already found a plastic bin of toys there and were down on their knees on the carpet, searching through the box as if they were positive it contained fabulous treasures.

"Did Miss Jill tell you it was all right to do that?" he asked, just in case.

"Uh-huh," Tim said. "If it's in here, it's okay to play with. She said."

"Glad to hear it." Mitch smiled more broadly as Jill reappeared. "Is Megan asleep?"

"Out like a light. She never even stirred when I laid her in the crib. If she's that easy to care for when she's *not* worn out I'll be surprised, but for now she's being a little doll."

"A very tired one." Mitch yawned. "Guess I should head for home and let you get some rest, too."

His spirits soared when Jill replied, "You must be as tired as the rest of us are. Why not just make yourself comfortable here? You can take a short nap on my sofa or in the recliner, if you like."

"I don't want to bug you."

She laughed lightly. "Trust me, Mitch. You won't be a bit of trouble." Her smile waned and she gazed at him tenderly. "I like having you around. It makes me feel—I don't know—safer?"

Hearing that, Mitch wouldn't have left her unless the lives of others had depended upon him the way they sometimes did when he was working. As far as he was concerned, he'd never had a better invitation to hang around than the one Jill had just offered. He was not going anywhere. No, sirree. And as long as he was on the premises he'd be able to keep her out of trouble. At least that was his primary goal.

The boys had eventually gotten bored with playing on the floor and had crawled up onto the sofa next to Mitch. Tim was clutching a handful of plastic toy soldiers and using the armrest at the other end of the leather couch for a pillow. Paul was cuddled up against the fireman's side as they all dozed peacefully.

Jill had used that opportunity to duck into her room and change into more comfortable, farm-appropriate clothing—jeans, a scoop-neck T-shirt and sneakers.

She'd kept tiptoeing into the back bedroom to check on Megan every fifteen or twenty minutes because she wasn't sure how the child would react when she awoke in a strange place. Plus, she didn't want the nap to go on for so long that the little girl couldn't sleep later. She'd made that mistake with some of the first children she'd fostered and it had resulted in some very long, very trying nights.

Quietly passing the sofa she noted that Mitch was snoring. How cute he looked sleeping that way, with his head tilted back and his lips slightly parted. For an instant she imagined herself bending over him and kissing him awake.

The mere thought made her blush. Where had *that* ridiculous idea come from? She and Mitch had long ago promised to remain friends, period. And although they were now quite comfortable in each other's company, he'd never even tried to hold her hand, let alone kiss her!

Mortified and deeply glad he could not really read

her innermost thoughts, she circled the hassock where he'd propped his booted feet and went once again to the bedroom to check on Megan.

The blankets in the crib looked jumbled. Perhaps the child was getting restless and was ready to get up, Jill thought as she peeked through the doorway. Good. It was nearly time to awaken her, anyway.

Silently approaching the crib, she smiled and lifted aside the rumpled bedclothes. Her eyes widened with disbelief. The bed was *empty*.

Jill immediately bent to peer under the crib then whirled, frantic.

"Megan? Megan, where are you?"

Two strides took her to the closet and she jerked the door open. Except for a few cardboard boxes of extra children's clothes that were stored there, the space was unoccupied.

Her heart raced, pounded, fluttered. She felt as if she couldn't draw enough breath to adequately power her body and brain. Toddlers had been known to climb out of cribs and it was possible Megan was an escape artist. That was the most likely scenario. The one she hoped and prayed was right.

"Dear Lord, help me," Jill whispered, continuing to thoroughly search that bedroom, then proceeding down the hall to the next.

She almost crumpled and fell to her knees when she flung open that door. A small, familiar blanket lay on the floor next to the window—the *open* window—as if the coverlet had been accidentally dropped in passing.

Jill knew what she was seeing but her mind refused to draw the necessary conclusions. In a house this old, forcing one of those thickly painted, wooden sashes open was difficult for a grown-up. Even a much larger child could never have budged it, let alone pushed it as high as it now stood.

Fear filled her. There was only one conclusion possible. Someone else had been in this room. Someone who didn't belong. And Megan was gone!

Panic-stricken, she took a deep breath and let loose with a bloodcurdling shout. "Mitch!"

Groggy, Mitch was on his feet before he fully realized what had awakened him. It took him a few more seconds to get his bearings.

Paul was still sleeping soundly. Tim had dropped the toy soldiers into his lap and was starting to sit up.

"Is it time to go shopping?" the boy mumbled, yawning and rubbing his eyes.

Just then, Mitch heard a second shout. He hadn't been dreaming as he'd first thought. That was Jill's voice. And it was coming from the rear of the house.

"Jill!" he shouted, on the move before he was fully awake. "Where are you?"

"In here!"

When Mitch entered the hallway and saw her, he understood why her response had sounded muffled. Both hands were pressed over her mouth and she was leaning against a doorjamb as if she were in shock.

He grasped her shoulders and held tight, forcing her to face him. "What is it? What's wrong? Talk to me."

"L-look," was all she managed to say.

"Look at what? What scared you?"

"I—I never dreamed…"

Mitch gave her a shake. "Pull yourself together and tell me what's going on."

As he watched her struggle to comply, he was growing more and more anxious. Jill was one of the most sensible, levelheaded women he knew. Anything that could take away her ability to properly communicate had to be deathly serious.

"Is this where you put Megan?" Mitch asked.

"No. Down there." Jill pointed with a trembling hand. "In the crib."

Mitch left her and raced to the open door of the other bedroom. There was a crib, all right. No one was in it.

He whirled and shouted, "Where is she?"

Through Jill's shuddering gasps he was able to make out one clear phrase. *"I don't know."*

That chilled Mitch so deeply he could barely think. No wonder Jill was overwrought.

"Did you look everywhere?"

She raked her long hair back with shaky fingers and grabbed a tissue, clutching it in her fist. "Not yet." She motioned to him. "Come here."

Mitch was beside her in seconds. The more he studied her expression, the more he realized she was not overreacting. She was truly terrified.

"Why? What have you found?"

"The—the window," Jill stammered. "It shouldn't be open like that. I never leave them open unless I'm airing out the house. And that one really sticks."

"You mean somebody else opened it?" His misgivings blossomed into full-blown panic. "You think they took Megan? Is that what you're trying to say?"

"Yes!"

Part of Mitch's mind refused to process that conclusion. After all they had already been through, this simply could not be happening. Serenity was a peaceful place, a haven from the kinds of threats found in more populated areas. Everybody knew everybody here. There was no one he could think of who would be so bold as to break in and steal a child this way.

Except for Natalie Stevens, he told himself, gritting his teeth and praying he was wrong. There had to be another explanation. After all, kids loved to play hide-and-seek. Maybe the little girl was teasing them.

He caught a glimpse of Tim's ashen face peeking around the corner. "I have a job for you and Paul," Mitch said. "I want you to help Miss Jill look, really carefully, and see if Megan is hiding and playing a joke on us. Will you do that?"

Tim's mop of tousled brown hair shook as he nodded rapidly.

"Good boy." Mitch looked to Jill. "All of you stay inside, stay together and search the house while I check the yard." Lowering his voice he meant his next statement for only her. "And call Harlan. Tell him exactly what we've found and that we can't locate Megan. Tell him we'll call back the minute we're sure she's not here."

Jill grabbed his arm. "Do you really think she's still in the house?"

He didn't answer. He didn't have to. They both knew that Megan Pearson had probably been stolen from right under their noses.

Making her way cautiously to the open bedroom window, Jill shivered in the chilly air as she reached into her pocket, pulled out her cell phone and dialed 911 to report the crime.

"Nine-one-one. What is the nature of your emergency?"

"This is Jill Kirkpatrick out on Farm Road 19. One of the Pearson kids is missing."

"When did you last see the child?"

"Maybe twenty minutes ago. She was taking a nap. Somebody kidnapped her."

"Did you actually see the child being abducted?"

"No, but…" She bit her lower lip. "I'm positive, okay? Sheriff Allgood was just out here a little while ago. He knows what's been going on."

"All right. Please calm down, ma'am, and stay on the line. All our deputies are busy right now. We'll send someone out as soon as we can."

Jill could barely speak. "I'm not going to stay on the phone and I'm not going to stay calm. I'm going to go look for that little girl. Tell Harlan. He knows how important this is, even if you don't believe me."

Frustrated almost to the point of anger, Jill ended the call. There was so much she didn't know. Couldn't possibly guess. Such as, how had anyone known about that particular window? Had they simply tried them all until they'd found a weakness in her safety measures? Or had they been casing the place before, maybe when they'd attacked Mitch?

She paused and peered out into the side yard, trying to form a clear picture. The exterior screen had been taken down and cast aside. A six-foot-tall forsythia bush that was in bloom next to the house had obviously been disturbed, too, because hundreds of tiny, yellow petals lay strewn on the ground at its base, the pattern extending onto the lawn.

Her jaw muscles clenched. Some of those flowers

had landed atop the discarded window screen, meaning they had been dislodged *after* it had been removed. Something had jostled the cascading branches, brushed against the delicate flowers and caused them to shed petals.

Filled with a sense of escalating dread she called, "Tim. Paul," and hurried toward the living room. "Where are you? We need to check the house together like Mitch said. Maybe you guys can get Megan to come out if she's hiding from us."

There was no response. She frowned. "Boys? Where are you?"

A quick look up and down the hallway showed no one. Hurrying through the rest of the house, Jill found Paul still half-asleep on the sofa.

With trembling fingers she touched the child's shoulder and gave him a gentle shake. "Paul? Wake up, honey. We have to go look for your sister."

The brown eyes opened, focused on her, then widened. "Where's my mama?"

"I'm Jill. You're staying at my house, remember?

"Where's Timmy?"

That was a good question, one she was about to pursue. "I'm not sure. Let's go look for him, shall we? He may have found Megan for us."

Although the five-year-old took her hand he lagged back, clearly unwilling to trust her to lead him anywhere. Rather than continue to struggle against his reluctance she simply scooped him up and perched him on her hip.

Calling, "Timmy? Megan?" Jill made her way from room to room, checking carefully while also chatting with Paul to keep him interested and hopefully distract him from sensing the depth of her anxiety.

The farther they went, the more they searched, the more disheartened she became. It wasn't a big house and she knew every inch of it. The children were simply not there.

Heart racing and head pounding, she carried Paul out onto the porch off the kitchen. There was only one person she could go to, one person she could trust and always rely upon no matter what. Mitch Andrews. And right now she could hardly wait to rejoin him and at least feel a little less alone in this terrible mess.

There was no sign of him anywhere in the backyard so she shouted, "*Mitch!* Where are you?"

His head popped through the open barn doorway. "In here. Did you find her?"

Jill was so distressed she could hardly speak, hardly bring herself to answer. "No."

"Then why are you out here? I thought I told you to…"

Jill saw his eyes narrow, his brow furrow. When he spoke again she knew he'd spotted her problem.

"Where's Tim?"

Her voice broke when she said, "I have no idea."

Mitch was beside her in seconds. Instead of berating her the way she'd expected, he circled her shoulders with one arm, steadied her and leaned closer to say, "Don't panic. He has to be around here somewhere. When did you see him last?"

She blinked to clear her head. "Um, when you did, I guess. You told us to stay together and I just assumed…"

"You figured he'd listen to me. I know. I did, too, or

I'd never have left you." He concentrated on the child she was still carrying. "How about you, buddy? Did you see where your brother went?"

Paul rubbed sleepy eyes and shook his head.

"He was still napping when I went to get him," Jill explained. "I don't think he has a clue about what's been going on."

As she raised her gaze to meet Mitch's she felt a stray tear slip out the corner of her eye and trickle down her cheek. "What're we going to do?"

"Wait for the sheriff. Meanwhile, we'll start another search. Harlan can take over when he gets here."

"Ha! Don't hold your breath. The dispatcher didn't take me seriously when I called 911. Who knows how long it'll be before anybody shows up?"

"I'll take care of that." Mitch gave her shoulders a parting squeeze, then took out his own cell phone and hit speed dial. "This is Andrews," he said with authority as soon as his call was answered. "I'm at the scene of a crime and we need law enforcement out here ASAP. Got that?"

Astonished, Jill waited until he was through briefly explaining the situation and telling the other party where he was before she asked, "What did you just do?"

"Used my influence," he said. "Fire and police share the same dispatch center. The sheriff is on his way."

Her eyes misted. "Oh, *thank* you."

Once again his arm slipped around her shoulder and he drew her close, including the obviously confused five-year-old in their shared embrace. "It'll be okay. Tim is just out doing his own thing the way he always does. I'm sure he's fine."

She closed her eyes for a moment, soaking up the

solace. Mitch was probably right. Tim was most likely nearby and simply acting the part of the protective big brother. But what about little Megan? Where was *she?*

Jill felt Mitch's gentle grasp of her shoulder and thanked God that she wasn't facing this current ordeal alone. She couldn't think of anyone whose company she'd have appreciated more than that of this stalwart man. And there was no one whose judgment she trusted more than his. If he said Tim was okay, then he was.

Taking a shuddery breath, Jill looked at her comforter. "I'm really afraid for the baby," she said softly, hoping Paul wouldn't realize she was referring to his sister.

When she saw the muscles in Mitch's jaw clench and felt his arm tighten around her shoulders she realized that she wasn't the only one who was desperately concerned. Her best friend was worried sick, too.

And since she couldn't turn back the clock and do anything differently, it was only a matter of time before everyone started to agree that this was all her fault. She certainly wouldn't blame them. She thought so, too.

SEVEN

Not only did the sheriff and two deputies show up in response to Mitch's call, Thad Pearson and Natalie Stevens had apparently gotten wind that there was a problem at Jill's farm and had also arrived, although in separate vehicles.

Mitch quickly pointed them out to Harlan. "Uh-oh. Here comes trouble."

"Just what we need," the sheriff grumbled. "You stay out of this. I'll handle it."

"Only as long as they lay off Jill," Mitch replied. "I'm not going to let either one of them berate her. She's suffering enough already."

"None of this is her fault any more than it's yours," Harlan insisted. He cursed under his breath. "Might as well blame myself at that rate."

"None of us dreamed they'd come back and take the baby," Mitch said soberly. "I was more worried about somebody sneaking around and setting off another bomb."

The portly, older man rolled his eyes. "Don't even suggest it. I'm still taking plenty of flack from Little Rock over the way we managed that crime scene at the airport. How were we supposed to know the whole thing wasn't an accident? By the time we'd figured it all out, there was so much evidence trampled and lost that the lab didn't have a lot left to work with."

"It's our job to put out fires and save lives," Mitch said. "The fire department can't worry about preserving clues, either."

"Yeah. I know. Chief Longstreet isn't any happier about the way things turned out than I am, but it's too late to do anything about it." He grimaced. "I sure hope we can lift fingerprints from that bedroom window or some place in the house."

"I'm not holding my breath," Mitch said dryly.

Nodding agreement, Harlan stepped forward to intercept the newest arrivals. Mitch decided to stay close enough to lend a hand, just in case.

Listening to the shouted conversation up ahead, he shook his head in disgust. The way Natalie and Thad were carrying on, Harlan's biggest problem was probably going to be keeping them from killing each other on the spot.

Mitch hadn't heard questionable language like that since his teenage years when his stepfather had still been alive—and most of it was coming from Natalie! Thank heavens the kids hadn't been given to her to raise.

"I want those boys brought to me this instant," she demanded, whirling to confront Harlan while pointing over his shoulder at Jill, who stood in the distance, still holding Paul. "If that woman isn't capable of watching even *one* child, how can anyone expect her to take good care of three?"

Thad spoke up. "No way. Anybody but Natalie. I

wouldn't trust her to look after a psychotic pit bull with a chip on its shoulder. She's the *last* person who should get custody of impressionable kids."

Mitch didn't like the single-minded look in Thad's eyes or the unyielding persona he presented. If he'd had to choose which of the two to confront, Mitch would have picked Natalie in a heartbeat. Thad was clearly a far more formidable opponent in more ways than one.

Harlan held up his hands and shushed them. "Simmer down, folks. I have everything under control here. You can both go home."

"In a pig's eye," Natalie screeched, lunging to try to bypass him.

Before Mitch could act, Thad had physically restrained her. His actions were so swift, so practiced, it gave Mitch a start. He'd heard about Thad Pearson being involved in several fistfights since his return from combat duty but seeing him in action was a real awakening. No wonder his local opponents hadn't stood a chance. There wasn't a good old boy in Fulton County who could match those moves.

Rather than object to the interference, the sheriff simply nodded at the ex-Marine. "Think you can convince the lady to leave quietly, son?"

"She'll go." Thad turned and frog-marched Natalie back to where they had both parked while she loudly berated him and everyone else within earshot. All he had to do was point to her car, however, and she got in.

Mitch breathed a sigh of relief and smiled at the sheriff. "If that guy wasn't so rough around the edges he might make a fair deputy."

"I know. I already talked to him about it. He turned

me down flat. Said he intends to pick up where his brother left off and run Pearson Products."

"Does he have legal rights to it?"

"Nope. That's part of the problem between him and Natalie, I reckon. They aren't willing to share. They both want full ownership."

"What about the kids? Won't they inherit?"

"If it was up to me, those kids would get it all. Trouble is, they'd still need somebody to manage the business for them. That means they might be stuck with their aunt and uncle for years, no matter what happens."

Mitch shook his head and set his jaw. "The judge already appointed a special advocate to speak for them in court. Jill says the program is called CASA."

"Right. And the sooner the estate is settled, the better, if you ask me."

He paused to watch Natalie's car drive away. Instead of following her, however, Thad returned. His gaze was narrowed beneath dark, furrowed brows.

Mitch saw Harlan casually shift to rest his palm on the butt of his revolver before he said, "I meant you, too, Thad."

"I know. I'll go in a minute. I just want to ask about Megan. Is she really missing like we'd heard?"

"For the moment. But we'll find her. I've already put out an Amber Alert. Her picture'll be all over the news tonight. And I'm fixin' to call in extra men and maybe search and rescue dogs to help us if she doesn't turn up soon."

Mitch could tell that the other man was conflicted. Finally, Thad said, "Okay. We'll do this your way for now, Sheriff. If you decide to use civilians, keep me in mind. I'm a pretty fair tracker. I'll do anything I can to help find her."

"Where can I reach you?"

"At the airport, 24/7. I'm trying to set up a temporary shipping system in one end of the factory. Most of the records were lost in the fire but I want to be back in business when new orders start to come in."

The two men shook hands formally before Thad headed for his old pickup truck. Mitch waited until he'd driven off before commenting, "I know that guy's reputation isn't very good but he does seem to really care about his brother's kids."

"Yeah, he does." Harlan blew a noisy sigh. "I sure hope that little girl turns up pretty soon. Tim, too. The longer they're gone, the more chance we'll never find 'em."

To Mitch's chagrin he heard a quick intake of breath coming from behind him. Jill had apparently approached unnoticed while he and the sheriff had been talking and had overheard plenty.

When she said, "I know," with such heartrending emotion, Mitch stifled the urge to reach out and enfold her in a comforting embrace. It had been bad enough that he'd put his arm around her shoulders twice in the past hour. Giving her another hug would really confuse their relationship and maybe ruin their otherwise stable, long-standing friendship.

"We'll find Megan," he vowed, purposely stuffing his hands in his jacket pockets to squelch the temptation to reach for her anyway. "Tim will wander back on his own before long. He's probably out looking for her just like we are. I know if my little brother Luke was missing that's what I'd be doing."

"I thought he was all grown up."

"He is. I was just trying to make you feel better."

"Well, it didn't work. I don't care what you say, this is all my fault," Jill lamented. "That window was always such a bear to open that I didn't bother locking it. To tell you the truth, I can't remember the last time I tried. For all I know, it may have so many layers of old paint on it the latch mechanism doesn't even line up. I wouldn't be surprised."

"Then whoever did get it open has to be pretty strong, right?" Mitch asked, staring blankly into the distance.

"I suppose so." She frowned. "You look like you're a million miles away. What are you thinking?"

"I'm not sure. There's something nagging in the back of my mind, something that flashed there for a second, then disappeared. I can't quite put my finger on it."

"Was it something you and Harlan were talking about just now? Or your family? Did it have something to do with your brother?"

"Beats me." Thoughtful, Mitch continued to scan the yard. Everything looked fairly normal except for the extra police cars. One of the deputies was poking through the bushes while another had apparently circled the house, probably to dust the window for prints. Good thing Mugsy wasn't underfoot or he'd be driving them all crazy.

Mitch's heart leapt. *That* was it! The little dog was probably still in the house but Salt and Pepper always made pests of themselves, especially when Jill was outside. So where had they disappeared to and when had they left? He couldn't be positive but he didn't recall their barking when the sheriff had arrived this last time. And they certainly hadn't sounded off at Natalie or Thad.

"Dogs!" Mitch shouted. "That's what I was trying to think of. The dogs. They're not here."

Wide-eyed, Jill pivoted. "You're right. Maybe they're following the deputies around."

"And maybe they went with Timmy or they're on the trail of whoever took the baby," Mitch added excitedly.

Jill cupped a hand around the side of her mouth and took a deep breath, preparing to shout.

"Wait! Don't call them back. Not yet. I want to be able to look in all directions before you do that. We need to see which way they're coming from in case they are with the kids."

"How?"

"Well, I could request the ladder truck from the fire station but it'll be much faster if I just climb up on your roof." He looked to the sheriff. "You coming?"

"Not unless Miz Jill wants a big hole punched in her attic. I'll send Boyd with you. He's plenty skinny."

"Okay." Mitch was already jogging toward the house. "Let's go."

Jill held her breath as she watched the hurried preparations. Getting onto the roof was a genius move even though it was a chancy one. The pitch was steep enough to shed snow and ice, meaning it wasn't easy to navigate.

She saw Mitch step off the top of the ladder and begin to walk. His boots slipped repeatedly on the asphalt shingles. Jill had to bite her lower lip to keep from making frightened noises every time he faltered.

With the worst part of the climb still ahead, he

dropped onto his hands and knees. By the time he reached the highest point and cautiously positioned himself at the peak, Jill was a nervous wreck. Nevertheless, she returned his wave when he finally gained the ridge.

Sitting astride it like a rider on a horse, Mitch faced east while Boyd mirrored him and looked west. They were both wearing baseball caps but Boyd still had to squint and shade his eyes because of the sinking sun.

Harlan had loaned Mitch a two-way radio. The minute he announced, "Ready," the sheriff signaled to Jill. "Okay. Let 'er rip."

She lifted the sheriff's battery-powered megaphone and began to yell into it. "Salt! Pepper! C'mon, boys. Supper's ready."

At first, nothing happened. She could tell by the way Mitch was swiveling his head that he hadn't yet seen any sign of the missing children or of her animals so she kept calling.

Suddenly, he waved, pointed and raised the radio to announce, "Over that way. One of the dogs is at the edge of the woods."

"Just one?" Harlan replied.

"So far. No. Wait. There's the other one."

"How about the boy? Do you see him, too?"

"Negative. Just the dogs."

"Okay. Get on down here while Boyd keeps watch. You and Jill can take her Jeep and cut across the fields. The dogs are used to that vehicle so they're less likely to run off again when they see it."

"Copy," Mitch said. "On my way."

Jill met him at the bottom of the ladder. She was empty-handed.

"What did you do with Paul?"

"I left him with Harlan's other deputy, Adelaide, when I went inside and grabbed my jacket. She's the one who pulled Natalie off you at the fire. Remember?"

"I thought you couldn't leave him with anybody."

"It's legal when it's a member of law enforcement and Paul seemed to take to her. I thought he'd get bounced around too much in the Jeep." She started to run toward the old, red, four-wheel-drive vehicle. "Get in. I'm driving."

When Mitch didn't argue she was surprised and relieved. She knew every inch of her farm and was by far the wisest choice of driver; she just hadn't expected him to relinquish control of the situation. Not now. Not that easily. And not when they were embarking on what she dearly hoped was a rescue mission.

The engine roared to life. Jill shifted into low gear and headed cross-country through the long, brittle, winter grasses and struggling saplings.

Her pastures were surrounded by a dense, hardwood forest with cedars encroaching at the edges where the sunlight was strongest. Once you got beneath the limb canopy, even in early spring before the trees had fully leafed out, the woods seemed much gloomier and more forbidding. If Tim had wandered in that direction he was probably frightened, especially now that the ranch dogs had deserted him and it would soon be dark.

"You never saw Timmy at all?" Jill asked, having to shout to be heard over the roar of the engine and the growl of the geared-down transmission.

"No." Mitch raised the radio and triggered it. "Boyd. Can you still see the dogs?"

The crackly response was negative.

"How about the boy?"

"Nope." There was a pause. "But you're pointed at the right spot. Just keep going straight 'til you get to the stand of cedars."

"*Then* what?" Jill yelled, darting a glance at Mitch to assess his mood and try to tell whether or not he was optimistic.

"Then we go on foot," he replied. "I hope you've been praying, lady. We're going to need all the help we can get, earthly and otherwise."

Thinking back over the past few hours Jill could not remember one moment when she had *not* been praying, at least in her mind. The farm harbored many places where a boy—or a kidnapper—might hide, and there was undeveloped hunting land abutting three sides of her property, as well.

Mitch pointed through the flat, narrow windshield. "There! See? Isn't that one of the dogs?"

"Yes!" The Jeep shot ahead, bumping wildly over the rutted ground.

A sagging barbed wire fence across their path finally stopped them. Mitch was out of the Jeep and running before Jill had time to shut off the engine and set the brake.

"This way. Looks like the whiter dog is trying to lead us in," he called over his shoulder. "Come on. Move it!"

Jill followed, paying no heed when her clothing caught and tore on the prickly, rusted metal fencing. "Please, please, Lord, help us find the children."

She knew her prayer wasn't polished and religious-sounding the way the ones in church were but she also knew that God didn't care how flowery a plea was as long as it came from the heart.

Hers certainly qualified. All she could hope was that it would be answered before something terrible happened to those innocent children.

Mitch plunged ahead, beating his way through the tangled undergrowth while Jill struggled to simply keep him in sight. She could have called for him to slow his pace but instead she ordered, "Go ahead. I know my way," when he paused and glanced back at her.

"You sure?" Mitch shouted.

"Yes. Go." She gestured with her whole arm for emphasis. "Go! Find those kids. I'll be fine. I'm right behind you."

She didn't want him to lose sight of her dogs and ruin their chances merely because she was having trouble keeping up. The belief that they had to be close to success was what kept her moving long after she would have gladly quit and collapsed onto the leaf litter covering the forest floor. Those children were out there. They had to be. It didn't matter if she was present when Mitch found them just as long as *somebody* did.

Finally, she couldn't take another step. Completely spent and gasping for air she bent over and planted her hands on her knees. Just a few moments of rest. That was all she needed. She didn't have to keep Mitch in sight to follow him. She could clearly hear him crashing through the brush and shouting back at her from time to time.

He'd find Tim and Megan. She knew he would. And by that time she would have caught her breath and be ready to join him to celebrate.

If she had not been exerting herself so much she might have noticed sooner how cool the air was becoming. Now that she had stopped, the change was quite evident.

She straightened. Looked around. There was a good reason for the chill. The sun was almost set, the wind was picking up and she could smell rain.

Shivering, Jill folded her denim jacket more tightly around her, glad she'd grabbed it before leaving, and took stock of her situation. She and Mitch had been in such a hurry to chase the dogs that they'd come away without flashlights. At least she had. And he was carrying the only two-way radio.

Well, so what? She wasn't going to stop him when he was hot on the trail of the missing children. If she did happen to lose her way—as she was beginning to suspect had already occurred—she would simply use her cell phone to summon help. Maybe the sheriff could even talk her home using GPS coordinates the way the good guys did in mystery novels or on TV.

Still breathing raggedly, her muscles quivering, Jill patted her pocket and realized with horror that the garment she had heard ripping during her passage through the fence had been her jacket. The barbed wire had caught and torn open one of her pockets!

She gave a sharp, cynical laugh. Terrific. That pocket had held her cell phone. Her only lifeline. Her connection to both Mitch and the sheriff. And now it was gone.

Much of her earlier bravado vanished in a heartbeat. There was no way she'd ever locate a tiny, silver-colored phone like that amid all these crackling, shifting leaves. Not unless it happened to ring long enough for her to return and pick it up—assuming she had a clue about the path she'd traveled to get to the place where she now stood.

Jill peered into the darkening forest around her and listened, hoping to hear Mitch or the barking dogs in the distance.

Instead, the sharp, cracking sound of a breaking branch came from close by.

Jill whirled. Held her breath. Listened to the rapid pounding of her pulse. That couldn't possibly be Mitch. It was coming from the wrong direction and was far too close.

So who or *what* was it?

EIGHT

Mitch assumed Jill was sticking close the way she'd promised. It wasn't until one of the dogs started limping and slowed its pace that he paused long enough to survey the woods behind him more carefully.

"Jill? Jill!"

Scowling, he peered into the shadowy forest, hoping to spot her and wishing she'd been wearing a bright scarf or something like that instead of muted shades of blue denim.

At his feet, Salt, the whiter of the two herding dogs, whimpered and held up a paw as if trying to shake hands.

"Let's see, boy," Mitch told the animal, checking its foot and finding no detectable injury. He straightened and patted it on the head. "You're okay. I'm tired, too, you big faker."

He continued to scan the woods, listening intently. He couldn't hear anyone or anything so he shouted, "Jill! Where are you? Answer me."

Before he could call to her again he spotted a flash of color. *Jill?* No! Pepper had gone on ahead and was now coming back. Beside him walked a very weary, very dirty, barefoot, seven-year-old boy.

Mitch grabbed Tim, pulled him into his arms and held tight, as though he hadn't really believed he'd ever see him again.

Closing his eyes, he thanked God in silence, then grasped the boy's thin shoulders and held him away so he could study his expression when he asked, "Why, Timmy? Why did you run away like that? You scared us to death."

"I—I have to find Megan. To take care of her."

"That's Miss Jill's job now," Mitch told the sniffling, penitent child.

Tim shook his head vehemently. "Uh-uh. No way. She didn't do it good."

Mitch was glad she'd missed overhearing that comment, although he was still concerned because she'd lagged behind. It figured. If he told her to stay away she was right under his nose. Now that he'd asked her to keep pace she was nowhere to be seen.

Well, that couldn't be helped. Right now he had other problems. "Why did you decide to come this way? Were you following the dogs or were they following you?"

"I was following *them!* I saw them running off and nobody would listen to me and…"

"Okay. I understand." Mitch lifted the two-way radio and broadcast, "Sheriff. I have Tim. You'd better send a team out this way. He says the dogs led him out here instead of the other way around. They're with us now but it's highly possible they were trailing the kidnappers. We may be close to Megan."

"The boy's okay?" Harlan asked.

"Yeah." Mitch was squinting, trying to spot his erstwhile companion through the trees and wondering exactly which direction he had actually come himself. "Listen, Sheriff, I'm kind of turned around out here and I know I'd never be able to find this exact spot again if I move."

"Fine. Stay there so we'll have a starting point for the main search. We'll come to you."

"I have another problem." Mitch swallowed hard. "I've lost track of Jill. I thought she was right behind me but there's no sign of her. It's starting to get pretty dark out here and the weather looks like it's going to take a turn for the worse."

"Copy. I'll head straight for you. Boyd can take a few of the neighbors and fan out. We've gathered a lot of volunteers since you left."

"Good. Bring some drinking water, too, will you? Tim's probably dehydrated."

"Okay."

Mitch could hear the sheriff giving orders in the background right before he reported, "We have the GPS coordinates on that radio I gave you. When was the last time you saw Miz Jill?"

"It couldn't have been more than a few minutes ago. I kept an eye on her 'til she told me to run ahead so I wouldn't lose sight of the dogs." He gritted his teeth as he remembered making that difficult decision. "I never should have listened to her."

Harlan chuckled wryly. "Take my advice, son. Don't ever let her hear you say that. Just sit tight. We're on our way."

"Copy."

Mitch dropped to his knees and hugged the still-trembling boy again. Timmy was probably in shock, or close to it, so his well-being had to take precedence over everyone else's for the present.

What Mitch really wanted to do was scoop up Tim and backtrack to look for Jill. He supposed he could have, given that the sheriff now had the coordinates for his present position, but since the kidnappers could be close by he figured it would be smarter to stay put. The small clearing they were in wasn't exactly defensible but it did give him a good view in all directions. Jill's dogs were standing guard. Therefore, there was far less chance of exposing Tim to added danger if they waited right where they were.

"Besides," Mitch muttered, "who knows if the GPS readings are accurate enough?" No machine was foolproof. He'd known more than one driver who had gotten lost following the disembodied voice from a personal navigational unit.

His sense of duty was under intense attack, his loyalties torn. Three separate people were depending upon him and he could only help one at a time. Since he had Tim in hand and the dogs were remaining alert, it made sense to do as the sheriff had instructed and sit tight.

The trouble was, Mitch's heart kept insisting that he find Jill. He had led her into the woods and she was his responsibility, just as she had been since his fire department rescue squad had responded to the call for medical aid at the Kirkpatrick farm and he'd found her husband beyond any earthly help.

The sense of obligation that had begun that day as a totally innocent connection had blossomed into something more. At least it had for him. He was beginning to see that far more clearly of late and it bothered him. A lot. Surely Jill must blame him, at least subconsciously, for the death of her husband. He certainly tended to do so whenever he thought back to that fateful day. Like he was doing right now.

"It's my husband. He's out there. That way," Jill had screamed, gesturing wildly as the rescue truck had slid to a stop behind her farmhouse. "Under those big trees. Eric was trying to cut one down for firewood and…"

Mitch had grabbed his gear and led the way at a run. Speed hadn't helped. Although he'd administered first aid it had been clear from the outset that no one could have saved the injured man's life. But that didn't change the fact that Eric Kirkpatrick had died while waiting for an ambulance. Jill had watched the whole thing. How could she ever forget, ever view Mitch as someone other than the man who had been kneeling beside her husband as he'd breathed his last?

They had no future other than as friends. Mitch knew that as well as he knew his own name. He just wished with all his heart that they had met under more favorable circumstances.

Jill wasn't totally panicked. Not yet. But she could feel her heart pounding and had a deep-seated urge to run blindly through the woods to escape from whatever creatures, human or otherwise, were out there with her.

She held her breath. Strained to listen. There was the occasional chirp of nocturnal insects and the flutter of wings. Since most birds bedded down for the night and she knew an owl's feathers made no noise in flight, she assumed she was either hearing passing bats or perhaps an early season whip-poor-will.

Considering the abundance of limestone caves in the

Ozarks and the number of native species of bats, that was by far the strongest probability.

Well, bats or no bats, she couldn't just stand there and let the night close in around her. Was it safe to call out to Mitch again? Suppose someone else was out there besides the two of them? Would she be giving away her position and putting herself in worse jeopardy? After that first crunch of leaves and dead branches she hadn't heard another thing.

"Father?" she murmured, peering at a tiny patch of dusky sky visible through the thin, upper reaches of nearby oaks. "Now what?"

It would have been comforting to have heard a booming voice from Heaven delivering precise advice. Jill chuckled at herself. God wasn't going to talk to her like that. Besides, He had better things to do than worry about a foolish woman who'd managed to get herself lost in supposedly familiar woods.

Then again, she did recall the scripture in the tenth chapter of Matthew about their heavenly Father knowing and caring when even a sparrow fell. That comparison made her smile. Any dumb bird would do better than she had. At least it would know where it was.

Huffing in self-disgust she assessed her surroundings. Hilly terrain masked the actual sight of the setting sun, although she could detect its glow in the distance. Therefore, that direction was west. Since she and Mitch had been traveling due east before they'd left the Jeep, she could either turn west and try to return to her vehicle or continue in the opposite direction with the goal of eventually overtaking him.

Sensibility had little to do with her decision, she realized, chagrined. Above all, she wanted to find Mitch, to know he was close by, to sense his genuine concern.

She wasn't kidding herself by imagining that he cared for her in a romantic way. She knew better than to do that. They had even gone so far as to discuss it when he'd begun spending a lot of time with her, so she was well aware of his pure motives.

"Please understand," he had said a few months after Eric's funeral. "The last thing I want is to visit so often that I damage your reputation in town, but the fact is, you need help around here. You can't just let the pastures grow wild. Once those oak and cedar seedlings get a little bigger I won't be able to bush hog over them and knock them down."

"I don't know anything about farming," she'd replied. "Eric was…"

She remembered the pained expression on Mitch's face and the way his jaw muscles had visibly tensed.

"Look. I can't change the way things turned out but I can at least lend a hand when you need me." Mitch had gazed at her intently. "Please? Let me?"

Jill hadn't known what to say other than, "Okay."

Later, more than once, they had reaffirmed their goal of friendship and nothing beyond. She'd truly believed that was all she'd wanted. In many ways it was still true. Loving and losing had been an intrinsic part of her past life and if she could guard against feeling that kind of pain again, she would.

Pressing her lips into a thin line and remembering, Jill shook her head. First, her mother had willfully abandoned parental responsibility. Then, her grandparents had refused to take in a half-grown child, resulting in Jill's placement in a long series of foster homes that she had mostly endured rather then enjoyed.

When she had fallen in love with Eric Kirkpatrick and they had married, Jill had thought she'd finally have a real home again. Looking back, she should have known that was an impossible dream, one that had ended with Eric's last breath.

If she let herself fall for Mitch—and she wasn't admitting that she might—she'd be right back where she'd started, with even less assurance of a stable future. His job required him to be ready to risk his life on a daily basis. What kind of security was that?

None, she decided with conviction. She wasn't a child. She could control her thoughts, could protect her tender heart from being broken again by purposely keeping her emotional distance from Mitch.

In the back of her mind was a niggling perception that it was already too late to avoid falling for the valiant fireman.

Jill ignored the silly notion. She was tough. Self-reliant. Independent. Twenty-eight years of life had made her that way and she intended to take full advantage of those hard-won strengths.

Right now, what she basically needed was to locate Mitch and her dogs, she reminded herself. She swiveled and peered to the east. It was darker in that direction but she'd be okay.

Eventually.

She took one step, then another. Behind her she thought she heard other footfalls echoing hers.

She stopped.

The sound stopped.

"Mitch? Is that you?"

No one replied.

"Mitch?"

Trying to convince herself that the unsettling noises were figments of her vivid imagination, she lifted a foot as if to stride, then halted before actually bringing it to the ground.

To her surprise and horror, a crunch of dry leaves sounded at the very moment she would have stepped down!

Her eyes widened. This was no game. There was someone else out there. Someone other than Mitch. And whoever it was, was definitely trailing her.

Her head whipped around. Shadows shifted. Was that a man's shape? There? No, over there?

Jill crouched, ready to defend herself. Nothing moved except green, spring leaves in the treetops and a few dry ones that tumbled along on the forest floor, driven by the ever-increasing wind.

She turned to flee. Time seemed to be moving in slow motion. Lurching forward she leaned into the movement, her arms outstretched and groping to push aside intrusive vegetation.

A spider web brushed across her face and stuck, tangling in her flyaway hair. Stifling a scream, she whisked it away.

Her throat was dry, her breathing labored. She wanted to call out to Mitch again but the only sound she allowed herself was the gasping necessary to gather enough air to fill her lungs and keep going.

A dead branch crashed close by. She thought she felt the swoosh of its passing before hearing it hit the ground. Was it thrown? Swung? She didn't dare waste time looking.

Adrenaline had given her the strength to bolt and was maintaining her headlong rush among the trees. Feet flying, she paid no heed to the saplings springing back as she passed or the drier twigs that caught, tangled and tore at her hair.

A guttural voice cried out. Low. Male. Angry.

Jill knew her pursuer was gaining on her but she kept going. Kept praying. Kept running, stumbling and recovering, over and over. Her legs ached. Her lungs were about to burst. The landscape ahead swam in her vision like an out-of-focus photograph.

Suddenly, something caught the back of her jacket and she was thrown off balance.

"No!" she screeched, instinctively knowing she must not surrender.

A bulky, shadowy figure grabbed her wrist in a vise-like grip when she pivoted and tried to strike back.

"No! Let me go!"

She thrashed. Kicked wildly and swung at him with her free arm, hoping to somehow inflict injury.

Her imposing captor laughed as though he considered her resistance funny.

Anger added to the strength behind Jill's panic. She intensified her efforts. Her knee connected with the man's body and doubled him over.

He cursed and whipped the hand holding her wrist to one side, apparently intending to fling her to the ground.

That was all the opportunity she needed. Wrenching free, she rolled across the leaves and dirt, wincing when her ribs connected with a low, rocky outcropping.

She gained her hands and knees then pushed off,

struggled to her feet and stayed standing long enough to scramble away.

It didn't matter which way she went. Not anymore. Her wrist and arm ached and she had a stitch in her side but all she cared about was escape.

The curses of at least one man—maybe two—echoed.

That was a positive sign because the sound was fading as she put more distance between herself and the scene of the attack.

As Jill plunged through the dark woods she was hardly able to think, let alone pray. Nevertheless, she managed a breathless, heartfelt, "Thank You, Jesus."

Later, when she was sure she'd made a clean getaway, she'd ask God for directions that would lead her to Mitch. Right now, however, all she could do, must do, was keep running.

Rising, pivoting and listening to muted noises echo through the forest, Mitch took his cue from Jill's dogs. They had both perked up and started looking in the same direction, wagging their tails as if they were certain she was nearby.

"Praise the Lord," he whispered. "It's about time." He smiled at Timmy. "You stay right there and hold on to the dogs' collars so they don't run off."

"Why? Where are you going?"

"Nowhere. I just don't want to have to go looking for anybody or anything else. Not after the day I've had."

"Okay."

Mitch knew that Jill's big dogs could have easily pulled free from the boy's grasp. He also knew their temperament well enough to doubt they'd try unless they got the notion that one of their human flock was wandering too far afield and needed to be brought back into the fold.

The imaginary picture of Jill being herded out of the woods like a lost lamb and reunited with him and the boy amused Mitch. As far as he was concerned, that was exactly where she belonged. With him. He was in way over his head with regard to his feelings for her. The only good part was that she didn't know he'd broken his promise of platonic friendship. Hopefully, she never would.

Pausing, he listened intently. If he'd brought a flashlight he'd have signaled with it. Too bad they'd left her house in broad daylight and he hadn't thought to bring the right gear. Given his profession, that kind of mistake was inexcusable.

It was also understandable. They'd had little time to plan, let alone provision themselves sensibly. If they'd delayed they might have lost sight of the dogs—and then where would they be?

"Probably right where we are," he mumbled, feeling suitably contrite.

In the background, the boy was perched on a fallen tree, cajoling the dogs and holding on to their collars.

"It's okay," Tim crooned. "You be good. She'll come."

Mitch sincerely hoped the kid was right about that. He'd thought, judging by the earlier sounds, that Jill would have reached their position by now. Since she hadn't, he was wondering if it was safe to venture out a little way and look for her.

First, he cupped his hands around his mouth and called, "Jill? Hey, Jill. Over here."

There was no reply.

"Jill? Is that you?"

The lack of response when he'd expected one gave Mitch the shivers and made him more wary. *Okay.* He'd called to her. And she hadn't answered. *So now what?*

Mitch returned to Tim. "I want you to sit tight, understand?"

As more thunder rumbled in the distance he grabbed a stick and carefully poked the deeper leaves in the boy's vicinity to make sure there were no hidden, hibernating snakes. "If it starts to rain, crawl under this log and try to stay dry. I'll be right back."

"You said you wouldn't leave me."

"I'll be where I can still see you. That white dog shows up like a beacon, even in the dark."

"What's a beacon?"

"A bright light that leads lost people safely home," Mitch explained. "You know. Like you sing about in Sunday school sometimes."

"Yeah, okay. I know."

"Good." Mitch was anxious to venture farther away, yet afraid to go too far. Still, if Jill was out there and needed him...

Knock it off, he ordered, grimacing. According to Brother Logan Malloy, his preacher at Serenity Chapel, the Lord never gave believers tougher trials than they could handle. If that was true, he should be able to spot Jill without losing sight of Tim and the dogs.

"Yeah, right." Mitch took a deep breath and released it with a whoosh. He liked being in a position to help people. His chosen career proved that. But it was driving him crazy that he couldn't be in two or three places at once.

Lightning flashed. Thunder followed, muting the sound of something crashing in the distance. He thought he heard a squeaky, female shriek, then coarse voices that sounded anything but happy.

He shot a quick look at Tim and saw that the boy was following orders to the letter. He had not only shimmied beneath the fallen tree for shelter, he'd managed to drag the dogs most of the way under with him.

"Jill! Jill, I'm here," Mitch shouted, straining to listen to every creak and groan of the woodlands and hoping the mounting storm wouldn't cover her reply.

"Jill!" He pivoted and called in a different direction. "Jill…"

Thunder crashed. Raindrops the size of quarters began to pelt him. Mitch decided to rejoin the boy.

Then he froze. An unmistakable sound chilled him to the bone. It was a woman's piercing scream!

NINE

Jill was panting. Winded and spent beyond anything she'd ever experienced.

Thanks to the howl of the approaching storm she could barely hear her own footsteps, let alone keep track of whoever might still be trailing her, so she simply ran.

Branches overhead whistled and cracked in the strong wind, sending down showers of the previous autumn's unshed leaves in a tumbling, whirling mass. Large drops of rain were sparse, at first, then began to hit her with more regularity.

"The only good thing is that this will cover any noise I make. *And* get whoever is after me just as wet as I'll be," she muttered cynically.

If only she could be sure Mitch, Tim and Megan had taken shelter. She had to believe Mitch had located those lost children by now. The alternative was too horrible to imagine.

Rain began in earnest. It broke through the smattering of spring leaves as if they weren't even there. In minutes Jill was soaked.

She wiped her face with one hand while pushing

brush aside with the other. Visibility had been poor before. Now, the only time she could see where she was going was when lightning flashed.

The trouble was, that meant that anyone who happened to be behind her could also clearly see *her*.

"Stay there."

Without waiting for Tim to reply to his shouted command, Mitch plunged into the trees in the direction of the scream, detouring only when tightly packed stands of hickory saplings forced him to skirt them.

Night had fallen but thanks to the storm he was often able to catch brighter glimpses of the terrain.

One flash brought his heart into his throat. He hesitated, waiting for another and praying he hadn't been imagining Jill's blond hair.

He stared. Prayed. The flash repeated. It was her! And she was on the move, darting in and out of the shadows, her path erratic.

Mitch didn't spot anyone else, although judging by the way she was moving and glancing over her shoulder she obviously thought she was being pursued.

Since he had just called to her he figured she'd realize he was close by. When she started to bypass him, however, he lunged to stop her.

Jill reacted like a trapped tiger, mindlessly clawing and fighting.

"Hey! Quit it. It's me."

Something in her muzzy brain must have registered enough to bring her to her senses because she stopped flailing.

"It's okay, honey. I've gotcha," Mitch said. "You're safe. I promise."

The sky lit. He saw her jaw gape. Her eyes were so wide they looked unreal. She blinked. "T-Timmy?"

"He's safe, too." Mitch pointed. "He's right over there, under that big log with your dogs."

Jill went limp.

Mitch caught her up and returned to the clearing. The obviously worried boy was peeking out past his furry companions.

"She's okay," Mitch assured him. "She just got too scared and fainted, I guess."

"I ain't scared of nothin'."

"I'm *not* scared of *any*thing," Mitch corrected.

Tim beamed. "Yeah, me neither."

As Mitch gently lowered Jill to the ground he couldn't help noticing how lovely she was, even now. Her cheeks were smudged, her long blond hair was tangled. Wet strands of it were plastered to her forehead and cheeks, and her usually expressive blue eyes were closed. Still, she had never looked more beautiful.

Leaning over her to help shelter her from the deluge, he gently took one of her hands and rubbed it. Tim started to follow Mitch's lead, then apparently changed his mind about getting that wet and eased back under the log while the dogs crowded in to sniff Jill's shoes and try to lick her face.

"No. Go lie down," Mitch ordered, waving them away.

The moment Jill's eyelids fluttered his heart did the same. Half-awake, she started to struggle again.

"Whoa. It's me, remember?" He gently restrained her. "Take it easy. Don't be in a hurry to get up."

Eyes darting, searching, she was remaining a lot more panicky than he'd expected.

When she asked, "Where is he?" Mitch pointed to Timmy. "Right here with us. See?"

"No. Not him."

"Then who?"

Jill grabbed Mitch's hand and held tight, leaning on him to help her to her feet. She flipped her head to get her damp hair out of her face and finished combing it back with shaky fingers. "Somebody was chasing me. A man."

"The dogs didn't react to anything except you. That was how I knew you were coming. They got all excited."

"Somebody out there grabbed me. I'm positive." She stared at him as if she thought he doubted her claim. "I—I think I screamed. Didn't you hear me?"

"I may have. It was hard to tell over the noise of the storm." Mitch kept an arm around her waist, as much for himself as to steady her. "Now that we're all here together, I need to notify Harlan to call off the extra search."

"Extra search?"

"Yeah. For you. When you didn't catch up to me I asked the sheriff to send some men to look for you, too."

"What about…?"

Mitch saw her eyes glistening with unshed tears and guessed why. "Sorry. We haven't located Megan yet. But Tim was hot on her trail. Your dogs led him this far."

"Then we'll find her?" Jill's tone was half-pleading, half-exuberant.

"Of course we will," Mitch said as he grinned at the boy for emphasis. In his heart, however, he wondered how much time Megan had and who might have abducted her.

His first guess would have been Natalie Stevens but he figured a woman that small could not have raised the sticky window. At least not by herself. Plus, she wasn't the type to go hiking through a wilderness for any reason, let alone while carrying a toddler. No. If Natalie had been behind the abduction she'd had accomplices.

Thad could have managed the window, of course. He was certainly strong enough. Except he had no reason for taking Megan. He'd never sought custody of the children the way Natalie had.

Guiding Jill to sit on the fallen log, Mitch draped his jacket over her head like a cape while keeping his theories to himself. His main job was to look after her and the boy, at least for the present. Once Harlan arrived they'd discuss their next moves. Hopefully, Jill would be able to convince her dogs to return to wherever they had been trying to take Timmy.

If she couldn't get them to act, he didn't know what else they could do except go back to the house, wait for search and rescue and start fresh in the morning. That is, providing the rain didn't wash away the scent trail.

His gut twisted. Megan was out here somewhere, scared and maybe cold and hungry. They had to find her. They just had to.

By the time Jill, Mitch and Tim were joined by Harlan and the searchers, her dogs were acting so confused and so glad to have all these new playmates they didn't pay a bit of attention to commands.

"I'm sorry," she said, biting back tears of frustration

as she adjusted the loose-fitting hood of the disposable plastic poncho the rescuers had given her. "Salt and Pepper are herding dogs. They were never trained to track a scent. Whatever they did to get this far, they did on their own. I have no idea how to tell them we want them to keep going."

"It'll be all right," the sheriff assured her. "Now that we know where to start, we can bring the regular search dogs out tomorrow and pick up the trail from here."

"Will there be a trail? I mean, what about all this rain?"

"Those dogs can track a man through a raging river. They should still be able to work fine."

Jill's attention was diverted when Boyd suddenly emerged from the forest. He held up a black, knit cap, shined the beam of his flashlight on it and waved it for all to see. "This belong to any of you folks?"

Heads shook. Shoulders shrugged. No one claimed it.

Harlan looked pointedly at Jill. "You said you were being followed. Right?"

"Yes."

"Okay. Bag and tag that hat," he told his deputy. "It doesn't look like it's been out here long enough to get dirty so maybe it was lost tonight."

Jill's whirling thoughts centered on the sounds she'd heard. "I—I think the man may have fallen or run into something in the dark while he was chasing me. Maybe that's when he lost the hat."

"Let's hope so." Harlan claimed the packaged clue and gestured with his flashlight. "There's nothing more we can do out here. Let's head back to the Kirkpatrick place."

No matter how wet and miserably cold she was, Jill didn't want to leave. She grabbed Mitch's arm. "Maybe if we just look around a little more we'll find something, anything. Please?"

He shook his head. "No. You're exhausted and we have Tim to consider. He's not as wet as some of us are but it's not good for him to stay out in this weather. Besides, Paul is waiting back at the house."

"And," Harlan chimed in, "the last thing I need is a couple of amateurs clomping around out here and destroying what clues we may find come daylight. The more fresh scent you leave, the more confused the professional dogs will be. Think about it."

There was no way Jill could refute that logic no matter how desperately she wanted to. Harlan was right. She must put the children first and to do that, she had to follow the sheriff's orders, like it or not.

I don't like it, she reflected, disgusted, at her wit's end and on the verge of tears. The more she struggled to do things right, the worse the results seemed to be.

That wasn't true, of course. She had a favorite scripture in the book of Romans that taught: "All things work together for those who love God and are called according to His purpose." She just wished her heavenly Father would let her in on His plans, especially in this case.

Also clad in plastic now, Mitch used a borrowed flashlight to illuminate their way while he followed with Timmy.

Up ahead, others were breaking trail so Jill didn't have to wonder which way to go. It was comforting to see that the sheriff and his deputy were keeping guard on the periphery of the group in case there was more trouble. *In case my attacker is watching.*

Tim had recovered enough to be full of questions, especially now that he was warmer, thanks to Mitch's baseball cap, his very own plastic rain shield and make-shift boots that someone had taped around his ankles so they wouldn't fall off. "Where's Paul?"

Jill started to turn and answer when she heard Mitch reply, "Back at the house with a lady deputy."

"Oh." Tim paused, then added, "Will you stay with us, too, Uncle Mitch?"

"Sure. As long as I can. I'll have to go back to work soon, though."

"Take us with you."

Mitch laughed quietly. "Sorry, buddy. Can't do that. Miss Jill will look after you while I'm gone."

All she could hear after that was muttering. It was easy to guess that Tim was less than confident about her mothering capabilities. She didn't blame him. Given what had happened to his baby sister, she wasn't sold on herself either.

Her head was pounding and her leg muscles throbbed but she refused to ask anyone to slow down. As far as Jill was concerned, she didn't deserve any special kindness or consideration. She had blown it, pure and simple, and a toddler might have to pay the ultimate price for her negligence.

That thought burrowed into her heart and sent dag-gers of pain shooting through every nerve in her body. *No!* she wanted to scream. *No, no, no!* Not another loss for which she was to blame. Please God, not another one.

Tears began to stream down her face, making her

thankful that the darkness and rain hid her grief. She had been an imperfect daughter and her mother had abandoned her. She had failed to convince Eric that it was too dangerous to cut timber by himself and he had died as a result. Now she had been entrusted with the life of an innocent child and that child had been kidnapped.

Jill clamped her hands over her mouth to try to stifle a mournful sob that was rising from the depths of her soul and bringing with it all the anguish she was feeling.

She failed. The sound of her suffering reverberated as if the forest itself mourned.

Through her tears, Jill saw Mitch's light falter. Someone grabbed her shoulders. This time, she knew it was him.

He physically turned her around, drew her close and held her tightly.

She experienced the same sense of gratefulness she'd felt when little Megan had patted her arm, only much more so.

She didn't care why Mitch was hugging her, she only knew that she needed this reassurance the way a drowning victim needed a life preserver. Dying of thirst in a desert of grief and self-reproach, he was her drink of cool water.

"It's okay," he whispered. "It's okay, honey. I've gotcha."

Jill could not speak. She could only hold him, weep against his broad chest and thank the Lord she had a friend like this—someone who accepted her and supported her when even *she* had given up on herself.

* * *

Mitch closed his eyes and slowly rubbed Jill's back through her jacket and the plastic poncho. He had acted on instinct when he'd heard her crying and, given her response, he figured he'd done the right thing. At least he hoped so.

Some of the others had stopped to watch. That didn't matter. All he cared about was her. When she began to loosen her grip he did the same.

"I—I'm sorry," she said. Someone offered a handful of dry tissues and she accepted them.

"Nothing to be sorry for," Mitch replied. "It's been a rough day."

"No kidding."

He chanced a smile. "Cross my heart."

"I think I got you all wet."

"No wetter than I already was. Feel better now?"

"Actually, I do," Jill said, glancing at the group of searchers who had paused to wait while she dried her tears and regained her composure. "I suppose we'd better get a move on."

"Only if you're ready."

"Ha! After what just happened I imagine the smartest thing I can do is just keep putting one foot after the other and not let myself mull things over too much."

Mitch thought she might be trying to smile so he shined his light closer to her face. To his relief, she did look a little better—as long as he ignored the puffy eyes and reddened nose.

"Don't do that. I'm a mess." She blocked his view with her outstretched hands.

"You have looked better a time or two."

"More often than that, I hope." She gave him a shy, sidelong look. "Thanks."

"For what?"

"For just being you. For making me feel as if there really is hope."

"There's always hope," he said, sobering. He knew Jill had been referring to the missing child but he kept remembering how she had felt in his arms, how she had returned his offer of affection by slipping her arms around his waist, apparently without a qualm. Once she was back home and feeling more like herself, he figured she'd probably rue that natural response.

He knew he should be kicking himself for embracing her at all, not to mention doing it in front of all these other men. But he couldn't convince himself to be penitent. He had wanted to take Jill in his arms and hold her for a very long time. As far as he was concerned, he'd acted appropriately under the present circumstances.

What if there never was another perfect chance? Then maybe he'd make one, Mitch told himself. Something strange and wonderful had touched him when he'd been embracing Jill, and he was looking forward to finding out if he was simply overwrought or if there was more to it.

In the meantime, he vowed to remain her protector and do all he could to solve her problems, just as he had for the past several years. Then, when everything had settled down, perhaps he'd bring up the subject of their agreed-upon friendship. It was possible that he wasn't the only one who had sensed that they could become more than buddies if they let themselves.

He gritted his teeth and gripped the flashlight tighter. That degree of honesty would have to wait. He was no fool. He knew Jill's mental and emotional health hinged on the safe recovery of Megan Pearson. If that little girl wasn't found, alive and well, the heartbreak might destroy Jill's happiness forever—and his, too.

TEN

The Kirkpatrick farmyard was awash by the time Jill and the others arrived. The rainfall had lessened but water was still dripping off the eaves of the house.

Jill reached the covered porch and quickly pushed back the stifling plastic hood.

Following her, Salt and Pepper shook from head to tail, flinging water and looking mighty pleased to have almost all their charges corralled in one place.

Jill stepped to the porch railing and directed an announcement to the search party, "Please. Come in for coffee and whatever else we can rustle up. You all must be starved."

"Thanks, but not tonight," Harlan told her. "I wanna get plenty of rest and make sure everything is ready to go first thing tomorrow." He touched the brim of his cap beneath the bright yellow hood of his slicker. "We'll take a rain check. C'mon, boys."

The irony of his apt cliché made Jill smile in spite of herself. What was wrong with her? She should be down on her knees, face to the ground in prayer, loudly lamenting the loss of Megan while begging God's forgiveness. Yet she was still able to take small pleasure in the silliest things. In a way, she'd felt numb ever since she'd wept so fiercely back in the woods. Maybe there was no intense emotion left in her after all that.

Mitch joined her in two long strides, his boots thudding hollowly on the wooden decking as he stomped off mud and water. He had long ago begun to carry Tim and the boy was almost asleep in his arms. "Can't think of a better night for a *rain check*," he teased, smiling.

Deputy Adelaide came out the front door and closed it quietly behind her. "Glad you're back. I put Paul to bed about an hour ago. Then I searched the house again, top to bottom, just in case." She glanced at Tim. "Good thing you found that one when you did. This weather is clear nasty."

"Thank you for everything." Jill grasped her hand. "I don't know what I'd have done if Paul had been out there with us. It was awful."

She saw the dark-haired woman arching an eyebrow and eyeing Mitch.

"Somebody tried to grab Jill and she barely escaped," he said flatly.

Jill was delighted to hear the report of her ordeal phrased so positively. When she'd first told him about her set-to in the woods he had acted as though he didn't quite believe her. Perhaps Boyd's finding the lost cap had helped convince everyone, Mitch included.

"Praise the Lord you got away," Adelaide said. She checked her wristwatch. "Well, if y'all don't need me anymore, I'm going to report to the boss and see if he'll let me head on home. It's long past quitting time."

"Of course. And thanks again," Jill called. The deputy was already running for her patrol car, her jacket held over her head in lieu of an umbrella.

"We need to get inside and find Tim some dry clothes," Mitch told her. "We never did get any shopping done."

"I know. It's a good thing he's drowsy because I don't have any pj's for boys in his size. I didn't think to do the laundry so his are still dirty and smoky."

"Nothing much went as planned today." Mitch ushered her inside, closed the door behind them and wiped his feet again while Mugsy danced circles around the room. "Just make do with whatever you can find. Even just a big T-shirt will do in a pinch. I'll go give Tim a hot bath to warm him up, then put him to bed."

"Thanks."

"And, Jill," he added. "As soon as you dig up some dry clothes for Tim, take care of yourself, will you? You look terrible."

"Thanks. You're not so hot yourself."

He feigned hurt feelings so well, so dramatically, she had to smile again when he said, "Sure. Pick on me when I'm too tired to think of a clever comeback."

Jill sobered and shook her head. "How do you do it?"

"Do what?"

"Keep your emotions on an even keel when you're faced with the tragedies you deal with all the time as a firefighter?"

"We do the best we can in any given situation," Mitch replied. "That's all anybody can expect." He hesitated and gave her a look that was so empathetic it made her heart flutter.

When he added, "That's all any of us expect of you either, Jill," she was so grateful she wanted to throw her arms around his neck and kiss him.

If he hadn't been carrying the sleepy boy, she told herself she might actually have done it, too.

Mitch found pajamas for Tim, in a neatly folded stack of clothing, waiting just outside the bathroom door. He dressed the weary child, carried Tim to the now-secured bedroom where his brother already slept, tucked him in, then went looking for Jill.

He found her in the kitchen. She was clad in gray sweats similar to a set she'd left for him. Hers were decorated with embroidered butterflies while his bore the logo of a college football team. They both wore socks without shoes.

"Hi," Mitch said.

"Hi." She returned his smile, apparently without too much effort. "I see Eric's old clothes fit you. I thought they would. Did you get Tim settled okay?"

"Yeah." Mitch chose to concentrate on her question rather than think about whose outfit he was wearing. "I'd love to be there when he wakes up and realizes he's got on pink flannel pajamas with pictures of cute kittens all over them. He was so tired tonight he didn't bat an eye when I helped him put them on."

"Any little girl his size would be thrilled." Jill's smile widened. "We probably won't have trouble getting him to go shopping with us after that."

"No kidding. I hated to dress him that way but he had to have something warm to wear. I hung his wet clothes up in the bathroom to dry." Mitch was rubbing his own chilly arms through the fabric of the sweatshirt. "What are you cooking?"

"Omelets. We never had any dinner."

"Your Yankee roots are showing, lady. Around here we call it supper when we eat this late."

"Sorry. I wouldn't want anyone to disown you for associating with me."

"I'll take my chances. I'm surprised you're even on your feet, let alone fixing a meal." He got two mugs out of the cupboard. "Coffee?"

She nodded. "I made decaf. Hope you don't mind."

"Nope. I'm easy to please."

Mitch carried the steaming mugs to the white-painted kitchen table. When he asked, "Anything I can do to help?" and saw her tremble slightly he returned to stand beside her. "You okay?"

"No." Jill shook her head slowly. "One minute I want to scream and cry and the next minute I almost feel glad. It's like being stuck in a revolving door of emotion and not knowing how or when to step through."

"I understand." The urge to put his arms around her, to comfort her again, was almost more than Mitch could resist.

"You do, don't you?" She turned and lifted her eyes to gaze into his.

He was speechless. Was she asking for another embrace or was his imagination playing cruel tricks on him simply because it was what *he* wanted? He had no idea. Nor was he sure it might be wiser to ask rather than simply act on the impression he was getting. What if it was all wrong? What if he was misreading her actions and ruined their relationship by getting out of line? The thought of Jill refusing to allow him to continue to be near her was literally painful.

She reached to cup his cheek. Unshed tears filled her eyes, making them glisten.

Mitch heard his own sharp intake of breath before he realized he'd reacted so tellingly. Her gentle touch warmed him so thoroughly he lost the chill he'd been unable to shake since being caught in the rain.

He began to lift his hands slowly with the intent of pulling her closer. A tear slipped over her lower lashes and slid down her cheek so he paused to wipe it away with his thumb. In moments, he was thankful for the delay.

"I want you to know you're the best, truest friend I've ever had," Jill whispered. "I don't know what I'd do without you, Mitch."

Her hand lingered, caressing his cheek, and he let himself lean into her touch ever so slightly. Where he had envisioned romantic love, she had seen deep, faithful camaraderie. And she was right, as far as she'd gone. He did care about her that way. It was a truth they had often shared. It was also only the beginning for Mitch.

He forced a smile. "Don't worry. I'm not going anywhere. You're stuck with me, lady."

That brought a light laugh. Jill brushed away more tears and turned her attention back to her cooking.

The precious moment of intimacy, such as it was, had ended. The only thing Mitch was glad about was that he'd held himself in check long enough to hear what she'd had to say.

What if he had been dumb enough to try to hug and kiss her? That could have been catastrophic. They were so used to each other, so good at seeing into each other's hearts, there was no way he'd have been able to alibi his way out of a mistake like that.

Mitch turned away. His jaw clenched. He closed his

eyes and sighed quietly. No matter how long he lived he knew he'd never forget standing in the rain and holding Jill while she'd cried her eyes out. That might not be the kind of embrace he'd have preferred but since it was probably going to be the only one he'd ever experience with her, he figured it was well worth remembering.

Going over it in his mind, he realized he had also placed a kiss of comfort on her damp hair when the thin, plastic hood had slipped back far enough. Since she hadn't reacted at the time, he assumed she hadn't even noticed, which was just as well. But he had noticed. Oh, yeah. He had noticed plenty.

Right now, standing in her warm, welcoming kitchen and basking in the joy her presence always brought, Mitch had only one regret. He wished he'd kissed her more than just once when he'd had the chance.

Even if she never did realize what had happened, he would know. He would know.

They were just finishing their impromptu meal when Jill's house phone rang. She answered with a breathless, "Hello," and carried the portable unit back to the kitchen table with her.

"You don't have to sound so disappointed," the caller said.

"I'm sorry. I was hoping this was good news about Megan." Jill covered the receiver with her palm and whispered to Mitch, "It's the CASA volunteer, Samantha Rochard."

"You probably know as much about the missing child as I do," Samantha said. "The reason I'm calling is to prepare you. We have another hearing scheduled for the first of next week. Natalie Stevens is suing for immediate custody."

Heavyhearted, Jill nodded. "I suppose that's to be expected, although I had hoped the boys could stay with me in spite of everything that's happened."

"You still may get your wish," the advocate told her. "There's no guarantee that either of the relatives is on the up-and-up. Time will tell. In the meantime, the court may decide to let the children remain in your care. I'll certainly be recommending it."

Jill blinked back tears. "Thank you for your confidence. I just hope they find little Megan soon."

"Yeah. Me, too. I've been following the investigation through the sheriff's office. They're stumped. They said, at this point, even a ransom note would be helpful."

"Do you think there'll be one?"

"No telling. I know the sheriff has high hopes his teams will be able to pick up her trail in the woods tomorrow, though."

"You know about the dogs, then?" *And Timmy running away?* she added silently.

"I know enough to see that the children wouldn't have been one bit safer anywhere else. That's another fact I'm going to put in my written report to the judge."

"Thank you so much. I really do appreciate it."

"Hey, don't thank me yet. By the way, I'll need to know if you're planning to take new precautions to secure your home."

"Such as?"

"An alarm system?"

Jill covered the phone again and looked to Mitch. "She wants to know if we're installing an alarm."

"Tell her *yes*," he whispered. "I'm good with electronics. I'll either pick up the necessary components when we're in town tomorrow or order a system on the internet and have it delivered. That way we'll eliminate any wait for installation."

It occurred to Jill to insist that she could handle everything alone but it felt so good to have his support she kept that notion to herself. There was no harm letting Mitch help. After all, he was personally involved with the Pearson family and would naturally want to do what he could.

Besides, she admitted ruefully, she desperately wanted him to hang around. Especially while they were waiting to hear what had become of poor Megan.

The thought of that sweet, innocent little girl being dragged from her bed and taken who knows where made Jill's stomach lurch. Bile rose in her throat. She wished she hadn't eaten recently because the omelet was threatening to come back up.

"We'll—I'll get started on the alarm right away," Jill managed to say. "If you call here and don't get me, use my cell number. I'm taking the boys shopping for clothes and shoes tomorrow. They had nothing left after the fire."

Bidding the CASA volunteer goodbye and ending the call, Jill looked across the table at Mitch. Noting the added concern and empathy coloring his expression she forced a small smile.

"You okay?" he asked tenderly.

"I'll be a lot better once we locate Megan. For a moment there I think I stepped through my imaginary revolving door and got out on the wrong side."

"There's no sin in grieving," Mitch told her.

"But if I had a stronger faith…"

"I disagree. You did the best you could. God knows that. All any of us can do is trust the Lord to bring us through our trials in His timing and by His will."

"Funny you should put it that way," Jill said, blinking to quell unshed tears.

"Why?"

"Because I've known you for at least two years, and in all that time I can't remember once when I haven't heard you take the blame when things didn't turn out exactly the way you'd planned."

"That's different."

"Not from where I'm sitting." She assumed, judging by his stern expression, he was going to continue to argue.

Instead, he simply pushed away from the table and stood. "Want me to help you with the dishes or are you going to leave them 'til morning?"

"Leave them. Absolutely. I'd probably fall asleep at the sink if I tried to wash up tonight."

It had not escaped her that Mitch had taken exception to her candor and had pointedly changed the subject. Well, tough. She hadn't said anything that wasn't true. It was high time somebody told him he wasn't in control of the workings of the entire universe, even if he did keep acting as though he was.

"Why don't you curl up on the sofa again," she suggested. "I'll bring you a blanket if you want."

Mitch shook his head and raked his fingers through his still-damp hair. "I thought I'd bed down with the boys. There's plenty of room on the floor in their room and I want to be close in case of problems."

Jill's heart skipped. "We locked all the windows and doors. Do you really think they're still in danger?"

"I hope not," he said, eyeing her from head to toe. "But just in case, why don't you sleep in those clothes and leave the door to your room ajar so I can hear you call if you need me."

The underlying warning of his words sank into Jill's heart and laid there like an icy stone. He was definitely worried about the house being broken into again. And she should be, too, in spite of their precautions.

Fears that she had managed to bury in her subconscious had not only surfaced, they were making the fine hairs on her arms and the back of her neck prickle. Mitch was absolutely right. As long as the crime of Megan's abduction, not to mention the arson fire that had taken Rob's and Ellen's lives, remained unsolved, no one would be safe. Not at home. Not at church. Not even in a crowded grocery store.

She started for the door to the hallway. "I'll get you a pillow and blanket."

Although he reached for her arm as she passed, she noticed he didn't try very hard to catch hold. Instead, he simply followed her down the dimly lit hallway.

"I'm sorry if I scared you but you need to be frightened, Jill. Letting down your guard is the worst thing you can do."

"I know. I just hate thinking of so many awful things happening in Serenity. When I moved here I thought I was stepping back into a happier, less complicated version of a lifestyle that had disappeared from the big cities." She sighed. "Guess not, huh?"

"I still wouldn't want to live anywhere else," Mitch

said. "At least here you're surrounded by good people who look out for their neighbors."

"Not all of them do," she muttered as she handed him a pillow, then dug through stacks of extra bedding in the linen closet for a king-sized blanket and pillowcase. "There's somebody out there who has very different goals."

"Leave your door open," he reminded her soberly.

Jill nodded as she handed him the stack of bedding. "For once, I wouldn't think of arguing with you."

ELEVEN

Mitch had expected Mugsy to start to bug him as soon as he spread his bedding on the floor of the boys' bedroom. But once the little dog had sniffed his discarded, damp boots and had checked out the edges of the fresh blankets, he trotted down the hallway toward Jill's room.

Cute little guy, Mitch thought, smiling as he watched him go. He was glad Jill had both an inside companion and the dogs outside to stand guard. After they got an electronic alarm system installed and operating he'd feel even better, especially when the time came to leave her.

That outcome was inevitable, just as he'd told Timmy. Although Mitch planned to spend as much of his free time with Jill and the boys as possible, the fact remained that he had a regular job. Chief Longstreet expected him to pull his own weight, not ask fellow firefighters to sub for him indefinitely.

Pausing before lying down, Mitch checked each of the boys to satisfy himself that they were covered properly and sleeping. Apparently, the deputy who had put Paul to bed had also settled for whatever pajamas she could find because the younger boy was decked out in pink, too. Mitch smiled. Well, at least that way the brothers couldn't tease each other too much when morning came.

Morning. Sighing, he dropped to his knees atop the blankets on the floor and closed his eyes. It had been a long time since he had tried to pray this way and his mind was blank. He wanted to talk to God, to plead for Megan's return and Jill's peace of mind, but the proper words and phrases eluded him.

Perhaps he cared too much, was too close to the situation to make sense of it.

"I don't have to," he murmured. "God knows."

The truth of that simple statement settled in his heart and mind. Tranquility flowed over and around him. After more moments of silent contemplation, he simply said, "Thank You, Father," before crawling into his makeshift bed and wrapping himself in the blankets.

In a short time he was snoring.

Jill knew she should stop thinking so much. Knowing what to do and getting her brain to disengage were, unfortunately, not the same thing.

Part of her wanted to weep. Part of her couldn't help being glad that Mitch was staying and looking after everyone. Plus, Tim was back home, safe and sound. That was another praise, another reason to thank her heavenly Father.

The only real problem was Megan. Where could she be? And with whom? Who would steal a baby like that?

Many answers, all of them bad, occurred to Jill. If they assumed that the child's abduction had nothing to do with Rob's and Ellen's deaths, there were far too many other frightening options.

The biggest question was still, *why?* Perhaps if they knew that, they'd be better able to figure out where the little girl was now, which was probably why the sheriff had told Ms. Rochard that he was actually looking forward to receiving a ransom note.

Finally feeling the effects of encroaching sleep, Jill closed her eyes and kept silently repeating, "Keep her safe wherever she is. Please, Jesus?"

Letting her mind drift she slowly began to envision herself at the scene of the Pearson fire. She was searching, looking everywhere in her dream world for the children, even though instinct kept insisting they were somewhere safe. All she had to do was find them.

An unusual scent made her nose tickle. *Umm, smoke? A bad sign*, she told herself in her sleep. *Hate smoke. Smelly stuff.*

Something wet touched her cheek. It tickled. Jill's eyelids fluttered. There was another disagreeable odor wafting her way, something other than the smoke of her imagination.

She swatted at the tickle, then opened her eyes and nearly jumped out of her skin. She was nose to nose with her shaggy little dog and being treated to a close-up dose of panting dog breath.

Before she could order Mugsy off her bed, he barked right in her face. If his wet tongue and halitosis hadn't been enough to fully awaken her, that sharp, yipping warning certainly was.

Sitting up and struggling to see in the dark, Jill looked toward the window. Was that a glow?

The truth suddenly grabbed hold of her and made her

heart race. A fire? *Yes!* She couldn't see actual flames from her window but she knew *something* was burning. The wafting smoke odor she had thought belonged in her dream was now detectible in the bedroom.

She threw off her covers, screamed, "Mitch!" and hit the floor running.

Mugsy nearly tripped her trying to beat her out the door.

Bouncing painfully off the doorjamb didn't even slow her down.

Her bare feet slapped the hardwood floor and she caromed off the hallway wall.

"Mitch! Fire! Help!"

Awakened from a sound sleep, Mitch was disoriented for a few seconds before he realized where he was and what he was hearing. Kicking off blankets, he jumped to his feet just as Jill reached the doorway and flipped on the overhead light.

"I smell smoke," she said breathlessly. "And I think I see fire outside."

"You're sure?"

He was already stuffing his feet into his soggy boots but he looked up long enough to see her roll her eyes and arch her eyebrows before she said, "If I was dreaming, it was the most realistic nightmare I've ever had."

"Okay. You call 911 on your cell and head for the yard, just in case. I'll bring the boys."

"I'll help you. I can carry Paul."

Mitch picked up the younger boy and started to hand him to Jill before turning to the opposite bed.

He froze, staring. "Where's Tim?"

"How should I know? You were right here with him."

The accusing timbre of her voice cut Mitch to the core. He understood why she sounded so frenzied. He felt the same. Yelling at each other wasn't going to help so he tamped down his rising temper.

"All right. You take Paul into the yard and stay there. I'll make a quick pass through the house and join you. Holler if you see any sign of Tim."

"Right. You still want me to call the fire department?"

"No. Just take care of Paul. I'll make the call."

Without waiting to see if she was obeying his orders to the letter, Mitch grabbed his cell phone and hit speed dial to notify the station. As he explained the situation and gave Jill's address, he was tossing aside blankets from the beds and peering underneath furniture.

"No. I'm not sure," Mitch said in response to the dispatcher's questions. "But you'd better start at least one engine 'til I can take a closer look around. The homeowner said she smelled smoke. I'll call you back as soon as I know more."

As long as the electricity stayed on he knew he'd be fine. If there really was a fire and the overhead lines burned enough to cause a short, however, he'd be wandering around in the dark. That wasn't going to happen to him again. Not after the fiasco in the woods. He kept a heavy, metal light in his truck. That was his next stop. And while he was outside he'd be able to check on Jill and see whether or not she'd actually followed orders this time.

The power held. Continuing to shout for Timmy, Mitch reached the front door and threw it open. He was alone. It was hard to tell if he was seeing signs of a fire around the side of the house or if the interior lights were merely shining into the yard but something was odd.

He leaped off the porch and jerked open the door of his truck. Cell phone in one hand, flashlight in the other, he started around the side of the old farmhouse.

There! A pile of glowing embers! Jill was right. One small fire was smoldering next to the well house and another had been set beside a small storage shed. If the whole area hadn't experienced a soaking rain just hours before, either of those starts could have caused a lot of structure damage.

Mitch kicked at the closest pile of burning embers and scattered them enough to eliminate any danger. If these were the only two attempts at arson they'd be all right.

He spotted Jill standing next to the well house, balancing Paul on her hip and using a pitchfork in her free hand to try to break up that little fire. Her mop of a dog yipped at her and ran in circles, splashing water that remained in a few puddles.

"Here. Give me that. I'll do it." Mitch said. To his relief she passed him the long-handled tool.

"I thought I saw a fire over by the shed, too."

"Yeah. There was. I took care of it already."

"What's going on? Did you find Tim?"

"Not yet, but the house is safe enough if he happens to be hiding in there. Have you seen any sign of him?"

Jill shook her head and cuddled Paul, quietly assuring him everything was fine. "No."

"Okay." Mitch swung the beam of his light in an arc that encompassed the entire rear yard that lay between the house and the barn. "I'm going to call the chief and tell him what we've found so he doesn't start additional units. We need an investigator more than we need a second pumper at this point."

Just then he saw movement near the far corner of the barn. Timmy? Yes! The boy was moving so fast he was almost a blur.

Tim careened into Mitch. "Back this way." He shouted and tugged on the fireman's hand. "C'mon. Hurry!"

"Is there another fire?"

"No."

"Then take it easy. Everything's okay now."

The boy was adamant. "No, it's not. I saw somebody running away. Just like when…"

"Go with him," Jill said. "We'll be fine. I hear sirens already. Even if there is someone else out here they won't stick around. Not now."

"No. We're all going," Mitch ordered.

"But…"

"No buts. We're sticking together. I want a witness."

"Why?"

Mitch lowered his voice and spoke to her as privately as possible while Tim ran on ahead. "Because these fires are too amateurish to have been set by the same people who blew up the factory."

"Then who?"

He shrugged. "I hate to say it, but if I had to guess I'd be inclined to think Tim was responsible." He paused, hoping Paul's constant sniffling had kept him from hearing or paying much attention to the adult conversation.

"Why him?"

"Maybe to be a hero this time," Mitch offered. "I've seen situations like this before. He failed to save everybody when his home burned. By lighting little fires like these, he'd have the chance to alert us and atone for not being able to help his parents."

"You've already decided he's guilty, haven't you?"

"No. Not at all. I'm just saying it's a strong possibility."

"I don't agree."

"That's your prerogative. The evidence will prove it one way or another."

"Not if you never look beyond that poor kid, it won't," Jill insisted.

Mitch could tell from the stubborn set of her chin and the sound of her voice that she was more than disagreeing with him. She was irate.

"Look," he said, "there's no reason for you to feel you have to defend Tim. If he's guilty we'll get him professional counseling. He'll be all right."

"Good. Because after he learns that the one man he felt he could rely upon thinks he's an arsonist, he's going to need it."

Mitch didn't know what to say. He wasn't picking on Tim the way Jill seemed to believe he was. On the contrary, if the boy needed help, then this was the time for him to get it, not later, after he'd had time to develop into a true criminal.

"There!" Tim shouted. "See?"

Raising the beam of his flashlight, Mitch shined it across the pasture. All he could see was the boy, jumping up and down and gesturing wildly into the distant darkness, and Mugsy, gamboling after a scattering family of wild rabbits.

Jill was the one who asked, "What do you see, Timmy? Where? Show us."

"Over there…" The childish voice dropped. "He was right there. Running away. I saw him."

"Okay," Mitch said. "Now come with us. We need to wait out front for the fire engine."

Although Tim did obey, Mitch could tell he wasn't happy about the result of his supposedly meaningful discovery. That figured. Assuming the boy had started the useless fires, as Mitch suspected, he'd want to divert suspicion and make himself seem heroic by pointing out a villain. Even if there wasn't one.

Mitch doubted there had been anyone else around. He suspected they would find plenty of evidence that Tim had lit the childishly ineffective fires. Seeing that proven would be hard for Jill to accept but there was nothing Mitch could do about it. She was the kind of person who always saw the best in others, who viewed her glass as half-full rather than half-empty. That was one of her most endearing traits.

Leaving her standing aside with the boys, Mitch jogged up to greet Chief Longstreet.

"I think we're okay here, Jim," he said while the older man climbed out of his car. "I've seen barbecues that burned a lot hotter than these attempts. I kicked the coals away from the structures but we may want to wet down the exterior walls in a couple of places just in case."

"Arson?"

"Oh, yeah."

The chief shook his head and grimaced. "Great. Next you'll be telling me there was a bomb here, too."

"Not this time," Mitch said. "The Pearson fire looked like a professional job. This one was strictly amateur."

"Any suspects?"

"Afraid so." He gestured toward where Jill waited with the children. "I was sleeping on the floor right next to Tim but somehow he managed to sneak past me. We found him running around outside after all this started."

"Lucky you didn't sleep through it."

"Yeah. I guess Jill smelled smoke after the dog woke her."

"What dog?"

"Over there."

Pointing, Mitch noted that Mugsy was sitting at Jill's feet, sides heaving and tongue lolling. The others, however, were conspicuously absent. *Again.*

"Humph. I thought they were all right here," Mitch said. "We're missing a couple of bigger ones."

"You mean the two that took the boy into the woods and cost the sheriff a bundle in overtime wages?"

"Yeah."

His eyes narrowed and he shined his light into the pastures again, making a sweep with the strong beam. It was starting to look as if Jill may have been right to question his quick assumption regarding Tim's guilt.

He cupped a hand around his mouth and yelled to her, "Jill! Have you seen the other dogs?"

The shake of her head wasn't the only thing he noticed that made his blood run cold. In response to his query, Tim had started jumping up and down and pointing away from the house again.

This time, Mitch vowed, he was going to listen to the boy's tale, all of it, no matter how far-fetched it sounded.

And if there really had been an adult arsonist on the

prowl tonight? Mitch gritted his teeth. If so, he was going to have to make some very big apologies. Two of them.

For once, he'd be glad to be wrong.

TWELVE

Rather than go back to her own bed and try to sleep after everything that had happened, Jill had washed the mud off Tim's feet, and off hers and her house dog's, then had made herself comfortable in a rocking chair in the boys' room. She intended to stay where she could keep close watch over them for the remainder of the night.

She knew Mitch and one of his fellow firefighters had ventured into the pasture in search of her herding dogs and had eventually located them. Although the animals had been returning by that time, she strongly suspected that they had once again been tracking a prowler, probably the one who had lit the latest fires. No way was she going to leave the boys alone after that. Not for an instant.

Instead of hanging around in the yard and listening to the men uselessly speculating, however, she had chosen to take the children inside and put them back to bed.

The sun was just beginning to peek over the tops of the trees to the east when she yawned, stretched and gazed fondly at Tim for the umpteenth time. He had curled his thin body into a ball and appeared to be sleeping, yet his breathing was more rapid than normal.

She arose and gently touched him, stroking his thick, wavy hair and finding a sheen of perspiration on his forehead. Poor little guy. He acted so grown-up, so responsible, it was sometimes easy to forget he was only seven.

Tim opened his eyes, saw her and tensed. "Did they find Megan?"

"Not yet, sweetheart." Jill tried to calm him further with a tender smile. "I was just checking to make sure you were okay. How are you feeling?"

"Fine."

"Are you sleepy?" She guessed the answer to that question even before Tim shook his head.

"Then how about getting up and helping me with breakfast. I can use a pancake batter stirrer."

"Okay," he said, sounding hesitant. "But can I get dressed first?"

"Of course, if your clothes from yesterday have dried enough." She could tell by the way he was looking at the arms of his pajamas that he had noticed their decorations. "Sorry about the kitten pictures." Her smile grew. "Those pj's were all I had. I'm surprised you didn't object to putting them on in the first place."

Although a lopsided smile was the only response she got, she knew what Tim was thinking. "You only went along with it because Mitch was in charge, huh?"

Tim nodded vigorously.

"That's what I figured. He thought he'd fooled you because you were so tired but I knew you must have noticed. A kid as smart as you are doesn't miss a thing."

To her delight, Tim's countenance lit with a

face-splitting grin. His dark eyes twinkled. "I'm real smart. Mama says…"

Watching his elation fade so quickly touched her heart and made her reach out. "I know. This is hard," was all she had to say. Tim launched himself into her arms.

She embraced him and listened for weeping. There was none. The child simply held on to her as if he never intended to let go. Jill understood. She had felt every bit as alone, adrift and confused while growing up.

Sometimes, she still did.

Seeing that Jill had chosen to take his place as guard in the boys' room, Mitch had opted to spend the remainder of the night on the couch. He hadn't expected to be able to sleep well anyway. Not after being awakened so abruptly and then staying outside with the investigators until nearly dawn. Nevertheless, he had dozed.

Drowsy, he checked his watch and discovered it was almost seven. Since no one else seemed to be stirring he decided to tiptoe into the kitchen and start the morning coffee. The glass pot was just beginning to fill when Jill and Tim joined him.

"Good morning," Mitch said, studying her expression to try to determine if she was still mad at him for doubting Tim's innocence. It was hard to tell so he purposely kept his greeting brief.

"Morning. We're going to make pancakes."

"Yeah," Tim said, grinning. "I'm gonna stir." He cast Mitch a reproachful glance in passing. "And then Miss Jill is gonna take me shopping for real boy clothes."

"Ah, I see. Sorry about the pink pj's, buddy." He chuckled. "It was the best I could do."

"Uh-huh. You could of let me wear your sweatshirt to bed. I'm big enough."

"Almost," Mitch agreed as he caught Jill's eye. She was clearly enjoying watching him deal with the childish criticism. For that he was grateful because it had apparently helped her put aside any lingering grudges.

"So, what did you and the other men finally decide after I left you last night?" she asked. One eyebrow arched to punctuate the question. "Was I right, or was I right?"

"You were right," Mitch admitted ruefully. "We spotted a trail of wooden kitchen matches in the pasture. It looked like somebody might have stuffed a whole box into his pocket and not noticed they were falling out as he ran away."

"And…?"

Mitch shrugged. "That's about all. When the sheriff and the dogs get here today we'll have to be careful they don't take the wrong trail. Finding Megan comes first."

"Absolutely. But what if the same people are responsible for what happened last night?"

"Then we'll have an even better chance of locating her," Mitch said, pausing to tousle Tim's already messy hair. "We'll do it. I know we will. I promise."

In his heart he prayed he could keep that vow. While his logical side insisted there was a fifty-fifty chance of failure, his spiritual side kept telling him they had God in their corner.

Except there's no guarantee that the Lord will do things my way, Mitch argued, disappointed in his apparent lack of faith. It was one thing to wish for what he felt was right. It was quite another to convince himself to accept the opposite if that was how things turned out. He hated the helpless feelings he got when his best efforts seemed inadequate.

Sighing, he poured himself a mug of hot coffee and faced the window while he sipped it, pretending to watch the sunrise so he could hide the telltale moisture clouding his vision. It wasn't fair for an innocent child to have to suffer simply because there was so much evil in the world. It just wasn't fair.

Vivid imagination took Mitch where he didn't want to go and chilled him to the core. Suppressing a shiver, he forced himself to concentrate on visions of a successful rescue rather than on the possibility that physical and emotional injury might be taking place that very moment.

Why had there been no ransom note? Where could the little girl be? he wondered. None of this made sense. Then again, why ask for ransom when the child's parents weren't around to pay it?

That reasoning took him back to the original crime, the prime question. *Who killed Rob and Ellen? And why did the perpetrator choose to cause such devastation?* That was the real dilemma. So far, the official investigation was too lacking in conclusive findings to be of much help.

The only other idea Mitch could come up with was that there might have been some reason to want that office destroyed. But what? He was sure the Pearsons had been running an honest business, so why sabotage it?

"Maybe that's the answer," he whispered, thinking he'd kept the opinion to himself until Jill asked, "*What* is?"

"I was just thinking out loud."

"Fine. Tell me what's going on in your head and we'll compare notes. Two minds are better than one."

"Okay." Mitch refilled his half-empty mug and rested a hip against the tiled edge of the sink. He chose his words carefully since Tim was obviously listening, too. "I was wondering if it could have been the Pearson office that was the real target."

"Why?"

"Good question. What are some options?"

"Shipping drugs in the packages with the kitchen tools?"

"No way. You've been reading too many mystery novels. Those were two of the most honest folks I've ever known."

"What then?" Jill asked.

"A vendetta, maybe? Competition?"

"For what? The market for kitchen gadgets isn't exactly small. There should be plenty of customers to go around no matter how many firms offer similar things. Look at the crazy stuff they peddle on TV. If that junk sells, anything should."

"You're right." He stared across the rim of his mug, watching steam rise and letting his mind wander.

"How about other motives?" Jill asked.

"Such as?"

"I don't know. Didn't Harlan say that Rob had recently fired several men? Maybe one of them was upset enough to torch the place."

"Yeah. Farley and Bobby Joe Jones were caught gambling when they were supposed to be working.

And Vernon Betts was pushing seventy. He'd started making serious mistakes with big orders and costing the company thousands. I know Rob hated to let him go, though, because we talked about it at the time."

"Has Harlan checked all of those men yet?"

"He's working on it. So, what else can there be? Blackmail, theft, embezzlement…"

A squeaky gasp from Tim abruptly ended their speculation.

Mitch's eyes narrowed. "Is there something you want to say, Timmy?"

"Uh-uh."

Instead of insisting, Mitch looked to Jill and saw her clear comprehension. They now had a mutual goal. That clever child knew more than he was telling and it was up to them to convince him to open up, to trust them with whatever secrets he was keeping.

Jill smiled at the bowl Tim had been stirring. "Good job, honey. That batter looks just right. While I'm cooking the pancakes why don't you go wake Paul and help him get dressed?"

Judging by the way the boy's eyes darted from one adult to the other, Mitch assumed he was trying to make a decision. Might he be trying to muster the courage to reveal what it was that he was hiding?

"Tell you what," Mitch said, directing his comment to Jill although it was being made for the boy's sake. "Why don't I tag along and write down the sizes of clothes we'll need to look for when we go into town? That way we won't have to waste a lot of time shopping. I'd like to be back here by the time the sheriff's teams get done so we'll know what they found."

"Sounds good to me. I hate to leave home at all, even

though I know there's not a thing I can do to help—except maybe fix lunch for everybody."

Tim looked unhappy about the prospect of continued adult supervision but he didn't voice any objection as he turned and went to get his brother.

Following, Mitch paused next to Jill. "Is that okay with you or do you want me to stay and help you cook?"

"I can probably handle things out here. You're the professional firefighter. If you hear the smoke alarm going off you'll know I've burned something and you can take appropriate action."

That comment, as well as her tongue-in-cheek delivery, made Mitch chuckle. He lowered his voice and leaned close to her to whisper, "I don't want to give our little friend any more chances to duck out on us."

"I understand. And while you're at it, try to pick his brain." She cupped her hand around the side of her mouth, eyed the hallway Tim had just walked down and added, "That kid *knows* something. I can feel it."

Mitch had failed to get more than a few unintelligible grunts and shrugs out of the seven-year-old. Later, while they were all standing in the checkout line at the big-box store where they'd gone to shop for clothing, Jill had an opportunity to start a conversation of her own.

"What grade are you in, Timmy?"

"Second. My teacher says I'm real smart."

"I agree." Jill gave him a smile of encouragement. "I imagine you can read very well."

"Yup. Paul can read, too, but I do it better."

She pulled a glossy-paged magazine from the rack by the candy display. "How about this? Can you read it?"

Tim squinted at the place where she was pointing. "Sure. It says, 'Make your sweet tooth happy.' Is that right?"

"Perfect. How about this line?"

"Man con-vic-ted?" His quizzical gaze met hers.

"That's right. Go on."

"Man convicted of em...em... I don't know that word."

"It's embezzlement," Jill said, watching the child's expression. "Do you know what that means?"

Tim lowered his gaze and stared at the toes of his new sneakers. Jill and Mitch had decided to permit the boys to wear their new shoes out of the store, making sure to include the empty shoe boxes with their other purchases.

"Embezzlement is stealing," Jill explained. "It's really sneaky. You know it's wrong to steal, don't you, Tim?"

"Uh-huh."

"Have you ever heard the word *embezzle* before?"

"Uh-huh."

"When? Who said it?"

The boy cast a pleading glance toward Mitch, got no visible reaction, then turned back to Jill. "My daddy."

"When?"

"Just before...you know."

She could tell this was hard for the child but if it led to their finding his missing sister or the people who had killed his parents, it was worth pursuing. "Before the big fire, you mean?"

"Uh-huh. Mama and Daddy were yelling at each other. I just wanted them to stop. I didn't want anything bad to happen."

"We know you didn't, Tim." Jill put a hand of comfort on his shoulder. "That awful fire wasn't your fault. We all know that. It was a grown-up crime."

"But—but I could have helped. I saw the man and…" Tears overcame him and he began to weep.

"Do you think you know who it was?"

Tim nodded with tears streaming down his cheeks. Jill scooped him up and started for the door.

"We'll be out in the parking lot, getting some air," she told Mitch, eyeing their purchases in passing. "Can you handle this and mind Paul?"

"Sure. Go ahead. I'll put everything on my credit card." His brow furrowed. "Is Tim all right?"

"He will be. We all will be," Jill said. "I think we'll finally have something concrete to tell the sheriff." She gritted her teeth. *I just hope it's not too little or too late.*

Harlan's men had combed the woods in the direction the farm dogs had first led them, then had regrouped and followed the scent of the more recent arsonist. Neither trail had led to Megan or had turned up any sign of her.

Sitting with Jill and the sheriff at her kitchen table, Mitch felt as if he'd been punched in the stomach. "There has to be a connection," he insisted. "Did Jill tell you what Tim said this morning? Who he thought he saw at the time of the bombing?"

The older man wrapped his hands around his coffee mug and nodded solemnly. "She did. It's not exactly news. Rob figured somebody was stealing from the company. He'd already mentioned it to me and I'd briefed the police chief. Our problem was a total lack of proof."

Mitch leaned forward intently. "Rob must have had a good reason for his suspicions."

"If he narrowed it down he never shared his ideas with me. And, thanks to the explosion and fire, doing an audit is out of the question."

"Tim said his parents were fighting that night," Jill offered. "If there was a theft, why would they be at odds about it? I'd think they'd want to stick together to catch the criminal."

"Not if it was a family member or maybe an old friend," the sheriff said. "I've had my eye on Thad and Natalie. Vernon Betts, too, mostly because of all the unexplained losses while he was working at Pearson's."

"But why? How?"

"That's a good question. Natalie had better access to the company books, but Thad's the one who should know plenty about making bombs, especially considering the time he just spent serving in the Middle East. Trouble is, he had a solid alibi for the time of the explosion and so did she. No matter who the boy thought he saw, it can't have been his uncle Thad."

Mitch chimed in. "Natalie was a basket case over losing Ellen the night of the fire. And Thad was always very close to Rob. They were more like best friends than brothers. You can't really suspect either of them."

"I have to suspect everybody," Harlan said. "Money can do strange things to people."

"I still like the disgruntled ex-employees for the arson fire," Mitch countered. "So does Chief Longstreet. Tim might have been mistaken just because he was expecting to see his uncle in the vicinity."

"We're not ruling *anybody* out for sure. Now that

we've tried the tracking dogs and gotten nowhere, I think our best chance is the Amber Alert."

"And prayer," Jill said, trying not to choke up. "Lots and lots of prayer."

THIRTEEN

Jill and Mitch had discussed what to do with regard to the pending funeral for the children's parents and had basically come to an impasse. Mitch was dead set against involving the boys at all, while she argued that they deserved the chance to bid their mother and father goodbye.

Standing in her kitchen, washing the previous day's dishes while Mitch dried, she made sure the boys were occupied watching cartoons in the living room before reopening the discussion.

"Honestly, I don't know why you have to be so stubborn about the funeral. It's not going to be held in church, right? Brother Malloy is going to conduct the whole service for Rob and Ellen at graveside."

"That has nothing to do with it," Mitch responded.

"It has everything to do with it. I might feel differently if I thought the boys were going to get turned off about going to church after seeing the caskets sitting in the sanctuary. Visiting the cemetery won't hurt them a bit."

"I totally disagree," Mitch said flatly. "Kids won't understand what's happening and they'll either end up confused or traumatized—or both." His voice gentled. "Let them be innocent a little while longer, Jill. There will be plenty of time for them to see the world realistically after they grow up."

"That's the point," she said, shaking her head. "Now is the time for them to learn to accept loss—before a lot of complicated adult reasoning gets in the way. You said yourself that Tim talked about his folks going to Heaven."

"Yes. And that's a good thing. But it doesn't mean I think he's ready to watch a pair of caskets being lowered into the ground."

Sighing, Jill had to admit he had a valid point. "Okay. Suppose we talk to Tim and Paul about it and then make our decision based on their reactions?"

Mitch shook his head. "Uh-uh. Not when Natalie and Thad are likely to be at the cemetery. There's no way to predict what those two might do or say." He paused, frowning. "Besides, I'm not even sure it's okay to take the kids. Are you?"

"No. I didn't see any reason to ask Samantha to see about getting permission until we'd decided. I imagine she's encountered this problem before in her work with CASA so she'll know what's legal and what isn't." Thoughts of upholding the law immediately reminded her of Megan.

Blinking rapidly, Jill averted her face. If, Heaven forbid, Megan didn't live through her current ordeal, what would Tim and Paul do; what would they think? Perhaps Mitch was right. Perhaps it was best to leave them out of the actual service and take them to the cemetery later to visit their parents' graves if they seemed to need more closure.

She thought she'd managed to hide her emotional re-action until Mitch laid aside the dish towel and touched her shoulder. She didn't want to turn to face him. Didn't want him to see her misty eyes. Didn't want to admit how upset she still was over a crisis she should have turned over to God long ago. Either she trusted her heavenly Father or she didn't. It should be as simple as that. Only it wasn't.

"Look," Mitch said quietly, tenderly. "Try to put yourself in my place. I can't do anything more for Rob except protect his kids. We've both been trying to do that. And in spite of all our best efforts, we haven't been totally successful."

"You don't have to remind me."

"I think I do," Mitch said. "This isn't a simple prob-lem. We have to not only handle today's decisions, we have to assume there will be others in the near future that are just as difficult. Maybe more so."

Jill knew exactly what Mitch meant without him having to spell it out. He was thinking of Megan, too. And he was trying to say that he feared the worst.

Tears began to slip over her lashes and slide down her cheeks. She swiped at them with the back of her wrist until Mitch handed her a paper towel and she was able to cover her face, to mask the sorrow she knew he was sharing.

Suddenly, from the other room, a child's high-pitched voice echoed. "Megan!"

Jill and Mitch stared at each other.

"Megan?" Jill's jaw gaped.

Mitch sprang into action more quickly than she did but they reached the boys only moments apart. The television program had been interrupted for a news bulletin. Megan's picture was on the screen. It had been cropped from a family shot that Thad had provided so it was grainy and indistinct but Tim had recognized his sister immediately.

He pointed and jumped up and down. "Look! It's Megan."

Jill's reddened eyes met Mitch's and she saw her own pain reflected in his gaze. Turning away and blotting her tears with the paper towel, she took the coward's way out and fled back to the kitchen. Would this waking nightmare never end? Was it possible that no one would locate Megan, that she had vanished forever?

That thought settled in Jill's heart and made her ache all over. She gripped the tiled edge of the sink and leaned against it for balance. "Please Jesus," she prayed. "Please? Give us something. Anything."

Logic kept insisting that her efforts were futile while her faith did battle with doubt. She did believe in God, in Jesus. Really, she did. It was just so hard to accept those things for which she had no earthly answers.

Eyes tightly closed, heart racing, Jill was out of words, out of wishes, out of imagined, fairy-tale outcomes.

And now, unable to reason her way through this dilemma, she did what she'd truly wanted to do all along. She gave in and turned herself, her life and her currently needy loved ones over to the Lord's mercy and care.

By the following weekend Mitch was satisfied that his concerns about the upcoming funeral had been addressed. Jill had spoken with Brother Malloy and the wise pastor had visited her home to counsel the children. Apparently, that had satisfied Jill because she was no longer insisting that the boys had to attend the interment when it was eventually scheduled.

Regular Sunday school attendance, however, was another matter. One they could agree upon.

"I'll need to go home and pick up another change of clothes for tomorrow," Mitch had said Saturday evening.

Jill's expression had told him she wasn't thrilled to have him leave at all and that conclusion had warmed his heart. "I won't be long." Grinning, he'd gestured at his boots and jeans. "I know the folks at Serenity Chapel accept everybody, no matter how they're dressed, but I prefer to wear my best to church."

"Of course. I do, too."

"You look good in whatever you wear," Mitch had said honestly, enjoying the flush of her cheeks his compliment had produced.

"Thanks." She'd taken a step closer then and he'd wondered if she was going to give him the customary, Southern-hospitality, parting hug.

When she stopped short of putting her arms around him Mitch had waved to the boys and hurried to complete his errand. He'd been home several times since he'd started spending every free moment at Jill's but there were still a few things he needed to take care of, such as picking up his mail and making sure his apartment was secure.

On Sunday morning it took both Mitch and Jill to get the boys ready. Tim kept insisting he wanted to wear his new superhero shirt and whatever Tim wanted, Paul did, too. The compromise had been to allow the children to don their special shirts underneath their plain ones.

They escorted the kids back to their respective Sunday school classes, where their friends and teachers greeted them warmly. Because neither boy had wanted to be parted from his guardians, Jill stayed with Paul and Mitch with Tim.

They met up as soon as the classes were dismissed. Mitch couldn't help grinning the moment he spotted Jill. "Well, did you have fun coloring Noah's ark?" he asked. "We did. We even added drawings of Salt and Pepper to the other animals."

"Good for you. Every shepherd needs dogs like mine."

"That's what Tim said." Mitch felt the child take his hand. The gesture of complete trust warmed his heart every time it happened.

Jill was carrying Paul on one hip.

"Don't you think he's big enough to walk?" Mitch teased as they entered the sanctuary together for the worship service. He followed her down an outside aisle, greeting fellow worshipers and wishing them good morning as he passed.

"Only if I want to go everywhere at a snail's pace," Jill replied. "This kid is the exact opposite of Mugsy. Getting him to hurry is impossible."

"Okay. Give him to me." To his surprise, Paul tightened his hold on Jill's neck and buried his face against her shoulder.

"I think he's adopted me," she said, smiling and placing a tiny kiss on the top of the child's head.

Mitch knew her well enough to tell that the boy's newfound attachment was touching her deeply. She was not only holding him, she was also patting his back and speaking to him in a private whisper.

Entering an empty pew, Jill placed Paul on the bench next to her while Mitch directed Tim to join his brother. Taking the last place on the aisle, Mitch looked over at his companions. Although Jill was as pretty as ever, he couldn't help noticing another aspect of her character that impressed him greatly. In the space of a little more than a week she had become a mother to those boys as surely as if they had been born to her.

So what did that make *him?* Mitch wondered. Was he still playing the role of the kindly uncle as Rob had always implied? Or was he beginning to view the boys the way he might his own sons, assuming he ever had any?

That was an easy question to answer. It also made him decidedly uneasy. To anyone who didn't know their situation, he and Jill would appear to be a nice, normal couple raising two well-behaved children. Nothing more, nothing less. Yet they were far from it. They were merely temporary caregivers, and he wasn't even officially that. So why was it so effortless for him to imagine them as a true family? And what in the world was he going to do about it?

Nothing, Mitch decided firmly. No matter what he wanted for himself, no matter how much he cared for Jill and those orphans, this was not the right time to speak his mind and open his heart.

He knew without a single doubt that his duty was to see this ordeal through to its end, no matter how its outcome personally affected him; no matter how much it cost him to play a part for the sake of others.

Then Jill looked up and smiled directly at him, and all his rational convictions vanished in a heartbeat.

Although Mitch had to return to work on Monday, the following few days sped by for Jill. She was thankful that she had insisted on one new outfit for each boy that was suitable for church because those same clothes were perfect for court appearances, such as the one they were about to participate in, thanks to Natalie's ridiculous custody demands.

The brick-and-stone courthouse at the center of the town square was relatively quiet as Jill, the two orphans and the CASA volunteer climbed the stairs to the second-floor courtroom.

Sniffing, Jill wrinkled her nose. The place smelled like disinfectant and mildew, which was probably an improvement over the decidedly unpleasant aromas the hundred-plus-year-old building might have given off if no one had tried to clean and freshen it.

She paused in the anteroom and crouched to make sure both children were neat. Tim looked pretty good but Paul was sniffling so she took a tissue from her purse and wiped his nose.

"There. Ready?"

Shorter, dark-haired Samantha Rochard gave Jill a sisterly pat on the back. "Relax. They look great. Everything will be fine." She lifted her slim briefcase for emphasis. "I told you what I was putting in my report."

"I know." Jill straightened and smoothed her sweater over the waist of her matching slacks. "I just keep remembering what this kind of thing was like when I was a kid. I never knew what was going to happen. One day I'd be settling into a nice, comfortable rut and the next

I'd be packing my bags for another change, another move."

"That's too bad. The CASA program existed back then but it didn't go national until Congress passed a victim's rights law in 1990. Even after that it took a while to develop the kind of widespread coverage we have now."

"I sure wish I'd had somebody like you to speak for me," Jill said. "By the time I'd been in the system for several years I'd given up having anyone listen to my opinion." She began to smile wistfully. "I believe more than one judge referred to me as 'sullen.'" The smile broadened. "Can't imagine why."

"Probably because you'd surrendered. That's what I see all too often with the kids I represent. When they decide they can't win, they just quit trying. It's a form of self-preservation. Perfectly normal."

"The word *normal* has never described my life," Jill said with a chuckle. She was nervous about the hearing and exchanging silly banter helped keep her from dwelling on the looming ordeal.

It would have helped if Mitch could have been there too, but he'd been unable to prearrange more time off work, much to the Pearson boys' chagrin. Tim, especially, had been upset over the idea of probably having to make do without his real-life hero.

Jill had wondered if the boy was going to spoil things by acting up in front of the judge—until Mitch had taken him aside before leaving for work and had a heart-to-heart.

After that, although Tim had still not seemed happy, he had at least cooperated. And, given his influence with Paul, the younger brother was also on good behavior.

Samantha gestured toward the door framed by a metal detector, then grinned at Jill and the boys. "Everybody ready?"

"I hope so." Jill held out her hands and was thankful when each child grasped one. She stood tall and lifted her chin. "Let's go."

Instead of moving forward, Paul tugged on her hand. When she glanced down she noted his pained expression. "What's the matter, honey?"

"I hafta *go*."

Samantha chuckled. "Better take them both to the bathroom. I'll wait right here."

Jill thought she was hurrying but by the time she returned, Samantha was pacing and glancing at her watch.

"Are we late?"

"Not very. Come on. We don't want the judge to get upset."

Entering the small courtroom gave Jill a sense of déjà vu that made her shiver, made her stomach do flips and brought the taste of bile to her throat. Nevertheless, she persevered. This was no time to think of herself. These children were depending upon her for support. She wasn't going to disappoint them.

Natalie Stevens and a skinny, big-eared man in a gray suit sat at a long, rectangular table to the right. Behind them, in the rows of chairs that made up the gallery, Thad Pearson and several other townspeople were observing. Jill surmised that at least one of the women in the group was a newspaper reporter because of the camera hanging from a strap around her neck.

Trying to ignore everything else, Jill followed Samantha to a table opposite Natalie's. Pasting a smile on her face she nodded at the taciturn-looking judge as she helped the boys climb into the adult-size chairs. This time the judge was wearing the black robes of his office and they made him seem far less amiable than he had when she'd seen him in his office.

Samantha apologized for their slight tardiness, explained the reason and pointed out that a copy of her latest report was already in the judge's hands.

Jill sat down and began to pray, hardly hearing anything else that was being said. To her surprise and delight the hearing was completed in mere minutes.

While Natalie berated her attorney, Jill reached for Samantha's hand. "Thank you, thank you," she said, blinking back unshed tears. "I had no idea it would be so easy."

"It was this time. Each session is different." The CASA volunteer patted Jill's hand. "At least we won't be back for a while."

Puzzled, Jill frowned. "We won't?"

That question made Samantha chuckle. "You really do get freaked out in courtrooms, don't you? Natalie was just ordered to stop bringing frivolous suits. We won't be bothered again for at least three months. Maybe longer."

"I can't believe I missed that!"

"Neither can I," Samantha said, patting her on the back, then gathering up her paperwork and shoving it back into the briefcase. "Come on. Let's get out of here before somebody notices that your mind is in another world this morning and starts to question your sanity, too."

"Is that what won? Did you prove that Natalie was unstable?"

"Among other things." Samantha had been smiling. Now she sobered. "The decision was also based upon the chance that the other children may be in danger. You do understand that, don't you?"

"Oh, yes." Jill was nodding slowly and holding each boy by the hand as before. "I understand that all too well."

Just then, a bright flash blinded her. The young woman with the camera had edged closer while their guard was down and had just photographed the Pearson boys.

Samantha shouted, "No!"

Jill stepped in front of the children to shield them from another attempt. She needn't have worried. Before the reporter had a chance to try for a second picture Thad had grabbed her camera and was holding it out of reach while punching buttons on the back.

"Hey! You can't do that," the reporter shouted.

Thad didn't say a word. Jill watched him finally hand the camera back to the irate woman.

He didn't smile at anyone, but Jill imagined a kindred soul. She sure hoped so. She and Mitch could use all the help they could get keeping these boys safe.

FOURTEEN

Mitch was stuck on duty at the fire station, as he'd feared, while the hearing was in progress. The county courthouse was located a short half block away but he couldn't leave on personal business without the chief's express permission and, unfortunately, Jim Longstreet's arrival that morning had been delayed.

Mitch was pacing the sidewalk in front of the station and shading his eyes to look toward the court square when he spotted Jill and the boys.

He waved, excited to see her and hoping that the spring in her step meant a positive outcome.

Tim and Paul returned his distant greeting while Jill continued to hold each child by the hand.

Mitch totally understood why she didn't want to let go. If he'd had his way he'd have kept both those kids—and Jill—on a very short leash, figuratively speaking, of course.

As soon as they were closer, he jogged up to greet them. One look at the elation on Jill's face told him all was well. "You won?"

"We all won," she said. "Especially the boys. They

get to stay with me. Samantha says the judge told Natalie to stop wasting the court's time."

"Praise the Lord," Mitch said. "I think we should celebrate. I wish I could leave my post and take you all to lunch."

"We can send out for enough pizza for everybody, including the other firefighters, and celebrate that way," Jill suggested, glancing warily over her shoulder. "A pesky reporter has been trying to take pictures of us so we're better off staying inside, out of sight. Besides, Tim and Paul want to look at the fire engines and I promised them they could."

Sweeping his arm in a wide arc, Mitch invited them in. "By all means. We love to show off the equipment. I have several elementary school visits scheduled for next month. Have to get them in before the end of the term."

"Which reminds me," Jill said as she led her charges through the open bay doors toward the enormous red, white and chrome engines. "What do you think about putting the boys back in class? The judge recommended it and Samantha agrees."

His gut twisted. "I don't know. It seems kind of risky."

"We don't want them to fall behind a grade because they miss their end-of-year testing. Suppose I took them to school and picked them up afterwards, myself, instead of letting them ride the bus? That should be safe enough."

"Maybe."

Mitch took a few minutes to think over the situation while he showed the boys some interesting aspects of the closest engine and let them stand on the wide rear bumper.

Finally, he lifted them down and crouched to put himself on their level. "Some firemen used to ride back here just like that on the way to fires, but it was really dangerous. Now, we sit up in the cab with the engineer."

"Cool." Tim was grinning so widely his ears wiggled. Paul mirrored the expression.

"I always thought so," Mitch said with a complimentary grin. "Maybe you can join the fire department and help people when you grow up."

Tim shook his head. "Uh-uh. I'm gonna be a cop so I can find lost kids like Megan."

"Good for you." Mitch's gaze met Jill's and lingered. "The best way to get ready for that is to study hard and get really smart. That's why I agree with Miss Jill and the judge. You boys need to go back to school."

"Awwww…" This time, Tim was anything but overjoyed. Paul looked as if he was about to cry.

"I *loved* school," Jill piped up. "It was fun."

Mitch began to chuckle. "Well, it is a necessity if a person wants to make a good living." He winked at Tim. "Otherwise, how are you going to afford to buy all the pizza you want?"

"With sausage and pepperoni!" the boy said excitedly.

"See?" Mitch said, escorting Jill and the children the rest of the way into the station house by a side door. "Mention food and a hungry guy will forget everything else."

"Does that work for full-grown men like you?" she asked, meeting his glance with obvious empathy.

Mitch shook his head and answered directly from his heart. "Not always." His smile waned. "Not this time."

Jill dropped the boys off at school the following morning, walked each of them to class, spoke with their respective teachers and showed them the court order so there would be no misunderstanding about who was—and was not—authorized to pick up the children. She doubted that Natalie would try to interfere again, given the judge's admonition, but she wasn't taking any chances.

Instead of heading straight home, she then swung by the fire station. There was nothing new to tell Mitch. She simply wanted to see him, to feel the full force of his emotional support. Since he had to bunk at the station when he was on duty, he hadn't joined them for meals lately, except when they'd shared the pizza. His absence had really pointed up how much he had been contributing to the upbeat atmosphere at home, not to mention giving the boys fatherly advice.

Before entering Mitch's office she paused long enough to smooth her jeans and adjust her jacket over the soft, blue sweater she'd worn, knowing he liked that color.

He jumped to his feet the moment she peeked through the doorway. "Are the boys okay?"

Jill smiled. "Relax. They're fine. I just dropped them off at school."

He sank back into his chair as if he were a deflating balloon. "Thank goodness. When I saw you I thought…"

"I'm sorry. I should have phoned before dropping in.

I just thought it would be nice to talk to an adult for a change."

"Kids getting to you?"

Jill shrugged, continuing to smile. "Not really. But I hate to go home when I feel like I should be taking some kind of action. I can't sit around twiddling my thumbs while Megan is still missing."

"I know what you mean." He gathered a stack of papers, evened the edges by rapping them on the desktop, then dropped the pile into a drawer. "So, where shall we go first?"

"Go? I thought you had to work?"

"I've made arrangements for a more flexible schedule for the next week or so." He chuckled wryly. "I already owe the other firefighters so many favors I'll be an old man before I can pay them all back."

"If you're really serious about leaving, then let's go see Harlan. I've tried phoning him but he refuses to tell me a thing. They must have some leads, some idea of where to look. If you and I did a little snooping around, what could it hurt?"

"Maybe plenty." Mitch got to his feet and donned the navy blue baseball-style cap and zippered jacket that were part of his everyday uniform. "Still, it won't hurt to ask him. Last I heard he was waiting for test results from Little Rock."

"You mean about the bomb?"

"Yes. We can't go poking around in the actual fire scene, but nothing says we can't at least take a look at the other buildings. Since they've allowed Thad to go back to work, that part of the plant should be accessible to anybody."

"I don't know what we could possibly hope to discover that all those police investigators missed."

Mitch arched his brows. "Did you come here to argue or do you want to find something useful to do?"

"*Useful,* yes. Useless, no," Jill countered. "I can waste my time at home, by myself." Realizing how ungrateful that sounded she blushed and waved her hands in front of her as if erasing a chalkboard. "Sorry. Forget I said that. I don't know what's wrong with me. I wasn't implying that being with you is a waste of time."

"I understand. You're as worried as I am and it's made you edgy." He opened and held the office door for her. "After you, Ms. Kirkpatrick. Shall we take my truck or your car?"

"My poor old Jeep rides pretty rough, as you well know. Let's splurge and take your truck."

"Harlan's office first?"

"Absolutely," she said, following Mitch through the station and waiting while he explained to his chief that he'd be gone for an hour or so on personal business. Judging by the knowing glance Longstreet sent her way, Mitch had briefed him fully. She didn't mind. Her only concern was making sure that the powers that be didn't assume she was carrying on with the handsome fireman while the children were housed with her, because that might cause them to be removed on moral grounds.

Ha! Jill thought, feeling foolish and more than a bit cynical. There was less personal involvement between her and Mitch Andrews now than there had been before this whole tangle of events had begun.

He had continued sleeping in the boys' room when he could be there and had spent his off-duty, daylight hours doing odd jobs around the farm, such as install-ing the new burglar alarm and outside lighting. That was pretty much the extent of their interaction. She got more TLC from Mugsy than she did from Mitch An-drews.

She also *gave* the dog more affection, she realized with a start. Well, so what? Mugsy didn't keep telling her what to do and what not to do. Knowing that Mitch had her best interests at heart wasn't enough to make his overbearing approach acceptable. Yes, she appre-ciated his help. And, yes, she wanted him there to help protect the children. But she wasn't willing to let her-self be bossed around by a stubborn control freak.

That conclusion struck Jill as funny. She and Mitch were a lot alike, weren't they? They each had definite ideas of how things should be done and were both posi-tive their way was best.

Sobering, she thought of Megan. In this case, she'd force herself to make any sacrifices necessary to find that little lost girl. It didn't matter whose ideas were right. All she cared about was success.

Letting herself dwell on the wisdom of submission— or at least full cooperation—as she walked with Mitch to his truck, Jill sighed. Nothing must distract either of them from their ultimate goal. Absolutely nothing.

Her cheeks suddenly warmed. *Not even the over-whelming sense of his closeness or the way I react to the accidental touch of his hand or brush of his sleeve?* she asked herself.

No. Especially not something like that.

Jill knew it wasn't enough to simply admonish her-self; she must mean it from the depths of her heart. And she did. Only the more time she spent with Mitch, the more she wanted to spend and the greater her desire grew to know he was nearby.

Fear had to be the underlying motive, she reasoned. Her home had been violated, more than once, and she was reacting by reaching out to him for security.

Okay. If that assumption was true, then why didn't she yearn to see Harlan or Boyd? And why hadn't she relaxed after Mitch had installed the alarm, complete with motion sensors to light up her yard if anyone came prowling around again? They'd tested the systems and knew they worked, so what was her real problem?

The word *loneliness* popped into her mind. That was ridiculous, of course. She had been devastatingly lonely right after Eric had died but she'd recovered long ago. She had her farm, her animals, all the children she could handle and enough investment income from Eric's insurance settlement to carry her through comfortably as long as she didn't squander the principal.

Therefore, what could be disturbing her usual peace of mind so much? Jill cast a sidelong glance at Mitch as he joined her in the truck and slid behind the wheel. Her stomach fluttered. Her heart sped. Her already warm cheeks began to burn.

When he looked over at her and smiled, she knew exactly what was wrong with her.

She loved him.

Harlan offered little information other than to mention that the authorities still considered Natalie, Thad and several former Pearson employees to be "persons of interest." Other than that, and reports of possible sightings of Megan that had not panned out, there was nothing he seemed willing to divulge.

"What do you want to do next?" Mitch asked in disgust as they left the sheriff's office and got back into his truck. "Want to cruise Main Street?"

"That's probably as good an idea as any. I have until two-thirty before I have to pick up the boys. What I'd like to do is go looking for Megan." She frowned. "Did you get the idea that Harlan was keeping crucial details of the case to himself?"

"I certainly wouldn't blame him if he was. You and I are not exactly pros."

Bright, flashing lights behind them drew Mitch's attention and he eased his pickup to the curb to let the emergency vehicles pass. "Looks like the cops are going somewhere in a hurry."

"Can we follow?" Jill asked, sounding excited.

"No way." The disappointment reflected in her expression made him reach for his cell phone. He could have used the two-way radio he almost always carried but doing so would have meant Jill could have overheard both sides of the conversation. Choosing to keep it more private until he knew what was going on, he said, "I'll call dispatch and ask what's going on. Will that satisfy you?"

She pulled a face and gave him a lopsided smile. "Is that my only choice?"

"Yup."

"Then I guess so."

Chuckling, Mitch pushed speed dial and was immediately connected. He identified himself to the dispatcher on duty and adopted a casual demeanor. "Hey, how's it going, Elaine?"

"Fine," the young woman answered. "You can relax. No fire department calls."

"Funny," Mitch drawled, "I just saw a couple of patrol cars rip past me. You sure there hasn't been an accident up on the highway?"

"Nah. We got another one of those false alarms about the missing girl. It won't amount to anything. None of 'em have."

His hand gripped the cell phone so tightly his fingers began to throb. Schooling his features to try to hide what he'd heard, he realized the minute he looked over at Jill that he'd failed. Her eyes had widened and she was staring at him as if she'd read his innermost thoughts.

"Oh, yeah?" Mitch said, hoping he wasn't half as transparent in regard to the dispatcher. "Where this time? At the airport?"

"Nope. Closer in. Remember that old plating plant out on Highway Nine? Some hikers said they thought they heard a baby crying. Ridiculous, huh?"

"Yeah. Ridiculous," Mitch said. "Thanks. Catch ya later."

Ending the call, he stuffed the phone back in his pocket, shifted into gear, whipped the wheel to the right and floored the gas pedal. Tires squealing, his truck took off with a roar.

Jill braced herself and grabbed for his forearm. "What's wrong? Where are we going?"

"Just hang on and pray," he shouted. "We can't follow the police, but nothing says we can't take a short-cut and get there before they do."

"Where? Is it Megan? Did they find Megan?"

"All I know is they got another tip," Mitch said, keeping his eyes on the road rather than chancing even a momentary glance at her. "There's more than one way in and out of the suspected location. If Harlan and the others go at it from the front, there's a slim chance the bad guys may have a chance to get away. We're going to fix that."

"It *is* Megan. It has to be," Jill insisted. "This is our answer to prayer."

Mitch hoped, with all his heart, that she was right. He figured, given their location at the time of the dispatch and his personal knowledge of the deserted site, there was a fair chance they had been granted the opportunity to take part in their own redemption.

That mattered far less than the ultimate safety of the child, of course, but for Jill's sake Mitch prayed that this tip was the one they'd all been waiting for.

FIFTEEN

Jill was glad she had her safety belt fastened because even with that much restraint in place she had to hang on in order to remain fairly stable during the wild, bumpy ride along the rural roads.

"How much farther?"

"Maybe half a mile."

"I don't see the police or sheriff's cars anymore. Are you sure we're headed for the right place?"

"Positive." Mitch braked, slid the wheels and turned a tight corner onto a rutted, overgrown dirt trail barely wide enough for one vehicle to squeeze through.

"Where are we?"

"At the back entrance to the vacant factory. This access is not on any map."

"Then how can you be sure this is it?"

"Because I used to play around here as a kid. I also inspected the premises for fire safety before it went out of business a year or so ago."

She could tell by the way his knuckles were whitening on the wheel and his jaw muscles kept clenching that Mitch was not in the mood for more conversation.

That didn't stop her from having plenty of questions. "Is this where Megan is supposed to be?"

"Maybe."

"Then why are we stopping?" Jill demanded. Her hands pressed the edge of the padded dash as if she could somehow make the truck keep moving ahead by sheer willpower. "Go!"

"All I intend to do is block this escape route so nobody gets away. Sit tight. We'll know more soon enough."

"No! I'm not going to wait here while that poor little baby is in danger." She unfastened her seat belt and reached for the door handle.

Mitch lunged across the truck. His strong hand clasped her wrist. Held firm. "No."

"Yes." Jill stared at him, refusing to back down. She could tell when he decided to capitulate. His expression told her. So did the fact that he released his hold and started to inch the truck ahead again.

She rubbed her smarting wrist. Mitch hadn't actually hurt her physically. Her pride was what was bruised. Nobody, not even her best friend, was going to stop her from doing all she could to rescue Megan. If Mitch thought he was going to be able to convince her otherwise, he was fooling himself.

Jill strained to listen by leaning her head out the open window. She could hear sirens in the distance but couldn't tell if they were actually approaching. There was too much echo, too much interference from the hills and valleys, not to mention the groves of old-growth oaks and a few sycamores and cedars that crowded in on the edges of the dirt trail.

Her breathing was as ragged as it had been when

she'd been chased through the forest behind her house. Her heart was beating rapidly, pulsing in her temples and making her head throb.

Peering ahead she searched for something, anything, that might tell her what she desperately wanted to know.

"Okay," Mitch finally said, his voice so low she had to strain to hear. "This is the end of the line. I've brought us as close as I dare to the parking lot. If we go around that last corner up ahead we'll be spotted for sure."

When he reached for her this time, his grip was more gentle. "Wait for Harlan, Jill. Don't spoil everything by bursting in and ruining the element of surprise."

She knew Mitch was right. That didn't make waiting any easier. "I want to be there. I should be there when they bring Megan out. She's my responsibility."

"We don't know for sure that she's even here."

"She is. She has to be. God wouldn't have brought us this far if she wasn't."

The look on Mitch's face was unreadable, although it seemed to border on disappointment. How could he be so negative? Had he given up? Surely not.

"Look, Jill," he said quietly, "we don't know that this is God's plan. Just because we both want the Lord to use us to find her, that doesn't mean He will. Or that He has."

"Where's your faith?"

Mitch tapped his chest with his free hand. "In here. I used to think that as long as I was a good Christian everything would always go my way. I found out otherwise. Bad things happen that we have no control over. You said it yourself when you were lecturing me about not blaming myself for failure."

"That's different."

"No, it isn't. What we personally want is less important than trying to figure out how to please the Lord. And stay out of His way."

She wasn't buying Mitch's arguments. "Phooey. God gave us brains so we'd use them, not sit around waiting for the rest of the world to wake up and fall into line."

Wresting her arm from his grasp she threw open the door of the truck and slid out.

Thick weeds and brush at the edge of the road were as high as her knees. Muddy leaves slipped beneath her feet. She almost fell before she was able to regain her balance, push past the open truck door and start to follow the road ahead.

Of course Mitch was right behind her. She was sure he wouldn't let her go alone no matter how upset he might be. Even when he was furious with her, as he surely had to be by now, she couldn't think of anyone else she'd rather have watching her back and protecting her from whatever menace they were about to face.

If Jill had not been totally positive she was doing the right thing she might have hesitated, but there was no doubt she belonged here. And, grumpy or not, Mitch belonged with her. In a few more minutes, when he was forced to admit she was right, he was going to be as thrilled as she was.

Gravel crunched ahead as heavy vehicles rolled over it. That kind of distinctive sound had to be coming from the parking area Mitch had mentioned. They must be very close.

Jill ducked behind a massive tree and listened. Car doors were closing up ahead but not being slammed the way she'd expected. There were no wailing sirens, either.

Cautious, she stretched just far enough to peek around the oak, then turned and whispered, "The cops are there. I can see one of their light bars but it's not flashing. I think they're sneaking up on the building."

"Good. Now we stay put 'til they get done."

"It's okay. They can't see me." Instead of heeding Mitch's orders she darted to a closer tree.

"Stop. That's far enough." Mitch said. Following, he grabbed the back edge of her jacket and held on.

She was about to turn and give him the fiercest look she could manage when she heard a dull crack. Then another.

A metal door banged open at the end of the building. Men began to shout. The sounds that had been muffled while taking place inside were now clearly identifiable as gunshots. Varying pitch told her there had to be more than one caliber being fired.

Jill was yanked backward so suddenly she almost fell. Mitch pinned her to the tree, sheltering her with his body while the shooting continued.

Bullets impacted glass and metal, sending shockwaves through the otherwise quiet woods. The police cars were being hit! And she had been right in the line of fire before Mitch had jerked her out of danger.

She owed him her life, her well-being, and soon she would thank him. For the moment, however, she was too frightened, too shocked, to speak.

Eyes closed tightly, she was just beginning to appreciate the sense of protection Mitch's closeness was imparting when he abruptly left her.

She blinked and looked for him. He had stepped into

the middle of the road to block someone's path. Since it wasn't a police officer, it had to be of one of the fleeing criminals.

Instead of trying to evade Mitch, however, the man rushed forward and tackled him like a football player!

The shiny silver metal of a gun barrel flashed in the sunlight as both men went down.

Mitch made a grab for the hand holding the gun as they grappled and struggled.

Jill couldn't speak, couldn't even scream.

The gun barked. Twice. Time stood still. She thought she was going to be sick when she saw the darkly clad man push off, leap up and continue down the road.

Mitch lay on his back in the dirt, barely moving.

The gun battle on the factory grounds felt as if it had lasted forever. In reality, it was over in less than a minute. Jill supposed that was a good thing because she'd been holding her breath ever since she'd seen Mitch fall.

Mitch! Her heart tugged her toward him despite the possibility of ongoing mayhem.

She came in low, then dropped to her knees beside him as he began to stir. "Oh, Mitch."

His first words touched her deeply when he asked, "Are *you* all right?" She changed her mind the minute he added, "That was the dumbest stunt I've ever seen. I should have tied you to the big tree when I had the chance."

Jill didn't know what to say. Argument was out of the question, mainly because she agreed with him. It wasn't much fun hearing that low an opinion of her intelligence, though, even if she did happen to deserve it.

She figured Mitch was probably as scared as she was in spite of his macho attitude so she put aside her rancor and offered him her hand. "I take it you're not wounded after all. Want some help?"

Mitch grimaced and got to his feet without aid. "I can manage. Did you get a good look at the guy?"

"Not hardly. He was in your face, not mine. Do you know who he was?"

"No. I didn't recognize him. Is the shooting over?"

"Sounds like it."

"Then why are you standing here? I thought sure you'd be storming the place looking for Megan."

"I—I..." Jill's head whipped around. She hated to admit it, even to herself, but when she'd believed Mitch had been shot, every other lucid thought had instantly vanished. "I was just going," she finally decided to say. "You coming?"

"Yeah." He was dusting himself off.

Waiting until he stepped forward, she hoped she was successfully masking her terror. Right now she figured she'd be fortunate to even walk, let alone reach the parking lot by herself, and it was her fondest desire to hide that weakness from Mitch.

To her relief, he took her arm. The mere touch of his hand on her sleeve gave her strength. Jill figured she shouldn't complain that he was glaring at her and wincing with almost every step. At least he was still there. Still supportive.

They paused before making the mutual decision to show themselves. The sheriff's car looked unscathed but several of the others sported fresh bullet holes and fractured glass.

Jill found the added energy she needed to cross the

lot and confront Harlan as soon as she spotted him. "Was Megan in there? Did you find her?" she asked, breathless.

"Nope. No sign of her." He frowned, looking first at Jill, then at Mitch. "What are you two doing here?"

"I parked on the dirt trail in back so I could block it," Mitch said. "Just in case y'all had forgotten there was another way out." He was brushing more leaves and twigs off his shoulders as he spoke. "Some guy flattened me when he ran past us. Sorry I wasn't able to stop him."

"You're lucky I don't arrest you both for obstructing justice," Harlan said. He huffed and gave them a cynical look that reminded Jill of the way Mitch had looked at her. "I don't suppose you remembered to pull the keys out of your truck, did you?" Harlan asked with arching brows.

Jill's eyes widened and she saw the color drain from Mitch's face.

"Never mind," Harlan said. "He'd probably have it hot-wired by now in any case. Go see if it's gone like I think it is. If so, I'll put out an APB and maybe we'll get a break."

Penitent, Jill realized that the probable loss of Mitch's truck was as much her fault as it was his. Maybe more so.

She waited with the sheriff. Mitch wasn't gone long. The disheartened expression on his face when he returned was telling.

"Gone?" she asked.

Mitch nodded.

Harlan broadcast the vehicle's description and the general area where it might be by this time.

Jill stuffed her hands into her jacket pockets. What a morning this had been. *And still no Megan.* Nothing else really mattered except finding that sweet little thing.

Jill's plummeting mood was not only because they had been disappointed by reality, it was also because she'd been so wrong about God's intervention on their behalf. She'd been positive that they were going to be there when the child was rescued. Positive. And where had it gotten her? Nowhere, except maybe onto Mitch's list of the most clueless people he'd ever known.

There was only one thing to do. She forced herself to smile as best she could and stepped directly in front of him. "I need to apologize."

"Don't worry about the truck. It's insured."

"It's not just that," Jill insisted as she labored to keep the nervous quaver out of her voice. "It's everything. I might have gotten you killed back there."

"Forget it. I'm fine."

"Well, I'm not," she said.

If she'd been certain that he wouldn't shove her away she'd have moved even closer, slipped her arms around Mitch's waist and laid her cheek on his chest. Unfortunately, his somber, brooding expression had not changed except to deepen and she was convinced he was still very upset with her.

Jill knew that her days of not caring how Mitch felt had long passed, never to return. She was also sure that it would be wisest to leave him alone and let him get over his anger in his own time. Convincing herself to back away from him, however, was extremely difficult so she simply stood there, mute and motionless.

Suddenly, the decision was taken from her. Mitch

put out his arm and shoved her to the side, pushing her behind him as if trying to shield her.

Looking in the direction he was staring, she was as shocked as Mitch. The deputies were bringing three men out of the building in handcuffs. Two were rough-looking strangers. The other was Thad Pearson.

"What are those men under arrest for?" Mitch asked the sheriff.

"Illegal gambling. Apparently there's been gaming going on inside for months. If we hadn't gotten the false Amber Alert we might never have stumbled on it."

"Do you think somebody was trying to tip you off?"

"Maybe. Maybe not." He gave Mitch a lopsided smile. "Boyd's car's pretty shot up and the chief of police is planning to keep his people here for a while. This place is inside the city limits so it's his jurisdiction. Can I offer you two a ride back into town?"

Jill paused. "Are you positive there was no sign of any children here? Whoever reported hearing a baby crying must have heard something."

"Not necessarily. It could have been a sore loser's way of gettin' even by callin' the cops."

"Oh. I hadn't thought of that."

The light pressure of Mitch's arm around her shoulders was so welcome it brought unshed tears. He might be mad as a wet hen at her, yet he was still looking after her, still offering the comfort she so desperately needed.

She would have liked to have been able to properly thank him but she knew if she tried to speak and saw any pity or similar emotion in his eyes, she'd start to cry again. She'd done far, far too much of that already. Weeping didn't solve a thing, nor did it express her true emotions. What she needed to do was thank the Lord that no one had been hurt, in spite of her mistakes, and praise Him for the man who was willing to put aside his own feelings for the sake of others, including her.

Gratitude filled her. So did a sense of growing peace. Jill didn't care that that feeling made no earthly sense. It was enough to simply rest in it. For now.

By the time Mitch and Jill reached the sheriff's office the missing truck—and the thief—had been located and dealt with.

"Thanks," Mitch said, eyeing his vehicle. "I guess we can chalk one up for the good guys."

"More than one," Harlan said. "We've known there was gambling going on for a long time but this is our first bust. I'm hopin' it'll lead to more."

"What about Thad? Will he get to post bail?"

The portly shoulders shrugged. "Probably. Why?"

"Because, I heard he's been running Rob's business single-handedly since the fire. I'd hate to see it go under just because he's stuck in jail."

Jill piped up, "He wasn't responsible for the gambling, was he? I mean, he was just betting. Right?"

"That's how it looked to us."

"Okay," Mitch said. "Let me know if Thad needs bail and I'll see what I can do."

As they left the sheriff, Jill asked Mitch, "What are you planning?"

"I don't know yet. Thad had been coming to church with his brother fairly regularly. I thought I'd notify Logan Malloy and see if he wanted to make a pastoral visit while Thad's in jail." He smiled. "Sometimes falling on hard times can wake a man up to what's missing in his life."

"What about the factory? What will happen to it now that Thad's not working?"

"I don't know. I suppose I should ask him if he needs any help. Trouble is, I have no idea how to run the place and I don't know of anybody else who does either."

Jill nodded slowly, thoughtfully. "I suppose contacting Natalie is out of the question?"

"Humph. It would probably be better to shut the place down completely and wait for Thad to get out of jail than it would be to let her get her hands on it."

"I suppose you're right. I'm certainly not looking forward to running into her again."

Mitch rested his arm lightly around Jill's shoulders, taking care to keep his touch as innocent and nonchalant as possible, while he walked her back to her Jeep. "Don't worry. I'll be sure I'm with you the next time you go to court. I wouldn't have missed the last time if the chief hadn't been delayed getting to the station."

"I know. And thanks for everything."

His heart gave a lurch when she gazed up at him with such evident affection and gratitude. "My pleasure," Mitch said. Meaning to use humor to diminish the seriousness of the moment he added, "It was fun throwing you into a pile of leaves."

Her blue eyes widened and reflected the bright spring sky. Turning sideways, Jill placed her hand flat on his chest as she gazed up at him and said, "We both know you risked your life to keep me from getting shot, Mitch."

Instead of taking advantage of the opportunity to confess his deep feelings for her, he convinced himself to wait. Too much was happening. Things were moving too fast.

He and Jill had developed a strong friendship over the course of the past two years. Taking that camaraderie to a new level and changing everything in a matter of days didn't make sense. At least not to him. He was a logical man who thought things through. It was Jill who jumped into trouble with both feet and then wondered how to get out of it. His responsibility was to keep his wits about him.

Touching the brim of his cap, smiling and nodding politely, he distanced himself from emotional involvement by saying, "Just doing my job, ma'am."

Instead of the grin he'd expected in return, Jill looked surprised. Then, she abruptly turned away, climbed into her Jeep and slammed the door.

Standing there staring after her as she drove off, Mitch wondered if he looked half as befuddled as he felt. What in the world was wrong with her? She certainly hadn't been behaving normally lately. Then again, he supposed nobody who was involved with the Pearson family could remain unaffected by the ongoing tragedy.

Ideas forming rapidly, he waited until Jill was out of sight, then turned and entered the sheriff's office. He might not be an official part of the investigation into Megan's disappearance but he did have some rights. Anything pertaining to the original fire was his concern. So was whatever happened to the site in the future, as long as he allowed his imagination to stretch the truth some. Maybe he could convince Harlan to share a few more details or even allow him to speak with Thad now that Jill wasn't present.

Thinking of the parting look she'd given him, Mitch wondered if she'd been angry or confused or what?

He'd assumed she'd been sharing his lighthearted mood until she'd turned on her heel and stalked off. Women. There was no understanding them. After all he'd done for her, all the times he'd stepped up and volunteered, why was she acting as if she hated the sight of him?

Mitch's jaw muscles clenched. He had teased her about it but Jill had been right when she'd claimed he'd saved her life. That should have proved his devotion if nothing else did. So what was her problem?

SIXTEEN

As far as Jill was concerned the whole morning had been a disaster, ending with Mitch's offhanded comment about her welfare being nothing more than part of his job. She was too weary to rest, too angry to think straight and too upset to eat, although it was past lunchtime.

That didn't leave much else except going home and trying to lose herself in her farm chores until it was time to pick up the boys. She supposed she could do that. Or she could continue to drive aimlessly around town making useless wishes about locating Megan the way she had been for the past hour.

Nothing made sense, least of all the abduction of the child. The police had checked the alibis of every person involved in the case as well as running down nearby registered sex offenders. No leads had panned out. Not even the most distasteful ones.

Was it possible Megan was really safe and sound somewhere and being watched over by someone who cared about her? That was almost too much to hope for, yet Jill's mind insisted it was a possibility.

Of course it was. Anything was. But she was no fool.

She knew what the odds were. Every hour that passed meant a lessening chance that the toddler would survive. It was that simple. And there was absolutely nothing Jill could do about it. That was what hurt so much.

She had been traveling without meaningful direction, hardly noting what neighborhoods lay outside her Jeep. That's why when she saw that she'd subconsciously driven toward the airport, she was taken aback.

"Could this be a sign?" she asked herself. Chuckling in self-disgust, she answered, "Sure. Just like the gambling den was. Get real."

Nevertheless, she pulled off the road and cruised around to the back of the Pearson Products warehouse where the employees parked. There were no other cars present, which was not all that surprising considering Thad's recent arrest. If he'd been operating the place by himself, as everyone assumed, there would be no reason for activity.

Still sitting behind the wheel, Jill turned the key, then clasped her hands and closed her eyes. "Okay, Lord, here I am. Now what?"

She felt silly praying that way but she didn't know what else to do, where else to go. Had random chance brought her here or was there an actual reason for it?

A better question might be, was it important? Somehow she sensed that it was, although details totally escaped her. She'd already exhausted her imagination. There was nothing left but to turn to God and trust Him.

Her forehead rested against her clasped hands on the steering wheel. She closed her eyes. Birds called. Insects began to buzz. The sun streaming through the windows warmed her and made her drowsy as she prayed.

When her driver's side door was jerked open and a hand clamped over her face, she tried to scream.

Mitch kept his palm pressed over Jill's mouth until he was sure she'd realized it was him. "Hush." He frowned. "What are you doing here?"

"I could ask you the same thing."

"Keep your voice down," he ordered.

"Why?"

"Because Natalie is inside. I was on my way here to do a favor for Thad when I saw her car out front, so I hid my truck and walked over. I figured I'd sneak up on her and see what she was up to." His scowl deepened and he made no effort to look amiable. "Imagine my surprise when I found you lurking, too."

"I wasn't lurking," Jill insisted. "If you must know, I was praying."

"Here? Now?"

"Yes." Her brows arched. "Here and now. You aren't exactly the answer I was expecting though."

"You're imagining things again," Mitch said. He looked around, wondering if they'd been detected and coming to the conclusion he didn't dare send Jill away. Not if he hoped to accomplish what he'd come for.

"Look. There's no way you can fire up that noisy Jeep and drive it out of here without being heard. You might as well come with me."

"Don't sound so thrilled." Cynicism tinged her words. "I know! I can go in one way and you can go the other. That'll double our chances of sneaking up on her."

"It'll also double the chances of being caught. Are you familiar with the layout of the building?"

"Of course not." Jill pulled a face. "I suppose you are."

"Yes. I used to visit Rob often." Mitch stepped back to give her plenty of room. "Come on. And no talking."

"Did anybody ever tell you you're bossy?"

"Yes. You. Now hush."

The look of consternation on Jill's pretty face almost made him laugh out loud. If he hadn't been so determined to carry out his plans to secretly observe Natalie he might have given in to the urge to at least chuckle. Jill was not only as hardheaded as he was, she was every bit as courageous. Too bad she didn't have more common sense to temper her bravery.

They tiptoed up to the rear door with Mitch in the lead. He paused. "Okay. I got a key from Thad so we won't have to break in."

"When did you see him?"

"In jail." Mitch gave her the most intense stare he could manage. "Are you done talking?"

Jill nodded. Judging by the way her lips were pressed together and her face was flushed she was plenty mad. Good. As long as being peeved kept her quiet he was fine with it.

The key clicked in the lock. Mitch turned the knob slowly, deliberately, and eased the door open a fraction of an inch at a time. He felt Jill's hand on his back, almost pushing him, and wondered if she was going to be able to control the urge to rush headlong into trouble again.

Laying his finger across his lips he glanced at her

over his shoulder. His gaze met hers and sent a clear warning.

Once again, Jill nodded.

Satisfied, Mitch pushed the door far enough that he could see the darkened, windowless room that lay ahead. Off to one side, in the corner Thad had made into a temporary office, a beam of light blinked behind stacks of cardboard cartons. That had to be Natalie. She was apparently swinging a flashlight from side to side as she examined the makeshift records room.

Mitch pointed, waiting until he was certain Jill understood what he was going to do. Then he motioned at the cement floor where they stood.

She shook her head.

Mitch stiffened and gestured, insisting without speaking. He froze and waited for her to give him some sign that she was going to cooperate. Finally, she dropped her gaze, exhaled with a whoosh and nodded. Sort of.

That was all the go-ahead he needed. First he pulled the exterior door tight behind them, then gave his vision a few seconds to adjust to the lower light level. There were enough cracks where the metal walls abutted the roof that the enormous warehouse wasn't totally dark, even with the doors closed.

He was glad Natalie hadn't turned on the overhead lighting because the dimness facilitated his stealthy progress across the room, yet allowed him to zigzag past rows of packing and assembly tables without running into anything.

The closer he got to his goal, the easier it was to hear the woman muttering to herself. That was very disquieting. She sounded both frantic and adamant, with a heavy sprinkling of the same colorful language he'd heard her use before.

"Stupid, stupid, stupid," Natalie said. "What did you think you were doing, huh? Why couldn't you stay out of it? You and that goody-goody husband of yours."

Mitch thought for a moment that the overwrought woman wasn't alone. Then he realized she must think she was talking to her deceased sister, Ellen. He held his breath, listening.

"I told them you wouldn't be here. You never worked on weekends." Her voice broke. She sniffled. "Why did you do it? Why? You had plenty for all of us. I told you I had to have more. Why couldn't you just give it to me? Why did you have to die?"

Was she talking about the bombing? It sure sounded like it. Suppose she fully incriminated herself? Would he be able to prove it in a court of law? Mitch doubted it. Even though he had a sterling reputation it would still be Natalie's word against his. If she got a good lawyer or claimed insanity she might walk away unpunished. Rob and Ellen—and their kids—deserved more than that. They deserved justice.

There was only one thing to do. Mitch had to go get Jill and bring her closer so she could hear Natalie's ravings for herself. That way there would be two witnesses.

He pivoted to start back for her and was so startled he almost yelled.

She was standing right behind him. Grinning.

Even in the near darkness Jill could see consternation replace surprise in Mitch's expression. That sight, coupled with her nervousness, nearly made her giggle.

Mitch lightly pressed the fingers of one hand across her lips and pantomimed "shush," while pointing with the other hand.

Jill understood. She hadn't been standing there for very long but she'd already overheard plenty. Boy, had she.

Natalie's voice kept getting louder and louder, as if she were losing what little sanity she had left. The woman's grip on reality was clearly long gone.

"You promised to come to my house that night. Why didn't you?" Muttered curses followed. "It was Rob's fault. I know it was. I wouldn't have cared if he'd died but you shouldn't have gone with him. You were all I had."

Jill leaned closer to Mitch and was thankful when he embraced her. Hearing all this was answering many questions, although it was painful to realize they were listening to a tale of murder. Natalie had obviously lost whatever sense of right and wrong she had once possessed. That made her dangerous. Deadly. And at this point it was clear she felt she had little left to lose.

Sniffling continued. The rambling ceased. Jill snuggled close to Mitch and wondered what they should do. If they confronted Natalie there was no telling what she might do, particularly given her current mental state.

"Ah-ha! Got it!" she shouted so abruptly, so loudly, it caused both Jill and Mitch to jump.

The maniacal laughter that followed made Jill cuddle closer to him and lay her palm on his chest. His heart was pounding. So was hers.

She looked up at him and whispered, "What now?"

Mitch shifted, signaled with a sideways nod of his head and began to draw her backward. They had circled a long table and were about to duck behind it when a bright light blinded them.

Jill raised her hands to shade her eyes. Mitch sidled in front, between her and the work table. When she leaned to peek around him, she saw that Natalie held more than the flashlight. She also had a gun.

Raising his hands slightly, Mitch spoke in a composed manner that truly impressed Jill. How he could act so calm when a crazy woman was pointing a loaded weapon at them was beyond her.

"Thad asked me to stop by and make sure everything was locked up," Mitch said. "He's stuck in town."

Natalie cackled. "I know. I'm the one who got him arrested."

"Really?"

"Yes, really."

Although Natalie still sounded angry, she was also beginning to seem pleased with herself. When Mitch took advantage of that mood shift, Jill was so impressed she wanted to applaud.

"That was very smart of you," Mitch said. "How did you arrange for him to be there during the raid?"

"Easy. He thought he was going to catch me red-handed. Stupid goody-goody. He figured he'd be able to prove how deep in debt I was by just talking to those people. I could have told him he was wasting his time."

"So, you owe a lot of money?"

The light wavered. So did the gun. Jill could see the black hole in the middle of the barrel and she judged it to be a fairly large caliber. A .22 was dangerous enough. Heavier bullets would be even more deadly, especially at such short range.

"None of your business," Natalie shouted.

"Hey, it's no skin off my nose," Mitch said with a casual shrug. "After the estate is settled you should be able to sell this place and make a good profit, providing the kids don't inherit it all and cut you out."

Natalie cursed. "Those kids are nothing but trouble. I wish I could have…"

Jill waited, still hunkered behind Mitch and praying they'd get out of this alive. She knew what he was doing. He was baiting Natalie, trying to get her to talk, to reveal her convoluted thinking and perhaps give the authorities more ways in which to prove her guilt. It was a fine plan—as long as it didn't backfire.

"Well, at least you only have the boys left to worry about, right?" Mitch said.

Jill held her breath. Was he thinking that Natalie knew something about Megan after all? She'd had a solid alibi for the time of the kidnapping. So had Thad, although right now it sounded as if he was merely a scapegoat.

Natalie chuckled. "You have no idea."

"Sure, I do," Mitch began. He let his sentence trail off as if he meant to continue.

"No, you don't. Nobody does. They'll never find her. In another couple of hours she'll be on a plane and they'll never track her down. Not in a million years."

Megan's alive! Jill's sharp intake of breath caused Mitch to shove her farther behind him and grab hold of her hand. She didn't mind. Anything that helped her keep quiet at such a crucial time was fine with her.

"Why send her away?" Mitch asked. "If you wanted to get rid of her, why not just have her eliminated the way you did her father?"

"Because she was worth more to me alive," Natalie said, gloating. "I didn't sell her for as much as I'd hoped but it was enough to get me an extension on my loans."

"Gambling," Mitch said flatly. It wasn't a question.

"Of course. How do you think I knew about the game at the plating plant building?" She gestured with the gun. "Now, we're going to have another terrible accident and two prowlers are going to die. Get over there. Both of you."

Jill felt Mitch's grip on her fingers tighten. He was pushing down, toward the floor. Was he trying to tell her something?

She signaled back, giving his hand brief, short, downward tugs and saw him barely move his head in a nod. He wanted her to duck. But when?

"One thing puzzles me," Mitch said, still maintaining his veneer of nonchalance. "Why send Megan away on a plane and chance being discovered when they check her ID? I thought you were smarter than that. Why not just have somebody drive her to wherever she's going?"

That brought more wicked-sounding laughter. "Drive her? Ha! That's a good one. I'd like to see you drive her across the ocean."

Jill gave a barely audible squeak, then clamped her free hand over her mouth. Megan was not being adopted via the U.S. black market in babies as she'd first assumed. She was being sent overseas, perhaps to live a life of captivity that many women had claimed was worse than death.

They could not allow such a horrible thing to happen. Jill knew that. So did Mitch. But what could they do? How could they get away?

Suppose they separated? If she ran one way and he ran another, perhaps one of them would escape to take the news to the sheriff in time to stop the little girl from leaving the country. She should be easy enough to trace, unless she was being flown on a private jet. There couldn't be that many overseas flights leaving the states within the next few hours.

"Clever," Mitch said. "I never would have dreamed you'd ship her out like that. I suppose you got a lot more money for her than you would have by just peddling her to some childless couple around here."

"You'd better believe it."

"Too bad for Ellen, though," he added. "I can't imagine how much this will hurt her."

"Shut up. Don't talk about Ellen. Ellen's dead." Natalie was almost wailing.

"Is she? Did you see her body?"

"It got burned up. Everybody said so."

"Then why hasn't there been any funeral? Did you ask yourself that?"

The flashlight beam wavered. "I—I don't know. They said it was because of the coroner or something like that."

Mitch kept pushing on Jill's hand, urging her to bend lower behind him. She complied. The less he had to worry about her, the more likely he'd be to look after his own skin and not try to be a hero again.

"Ellen's under police protection in the hospital," Mitch claimed. "If you send her daughter away she'll never forgive you."

Jill knew lying was a sin. So was murder and kidnapping. As far as she was concerned, Mitch could be forgiven for any falsehoods that allowed them to rescue Megan.

"Ellen's dead!" Natalie screamed.

She threw the light at him.

Mitch ducked.

Natalie shot in his direction.

The sound of the bullet splintering the tabletop above her head made Jill give a tiny shriek.

Next thing she knew, Mitch was diving past her and tackling Natalie. Another shot echoed in the cavernous metal building. Then, all was still.

Rising, Jill peeked over the top of the damaged table. Mitch was standing and pulling Natalie to her feet. He now had possession of the gun.

"Call 911," he shouted. "And make it quick."

"Phone?"

"In my jacket pocket."

Trembling, Jill skirted the end of the table and approached on his left, away from Natalie. It wasn't until she reached to push back the side of his jacket that she realized he was bleeding.

"You're hurt!"

"Never mind me. Just dial," Mitch ordered. "We're running out of time to save that kid."

SEVENTEEN

The sheriff and one deputy burst into the warehouse with guns drawn.

"We're over here," Mitch shouted. "I've got Natalie. She confessed. It's all over."

"No, it isn't," Jill contradicted. "She's the one who kidnapped Megan. We have to act fast."

The overhead lights snapped on, making Jill's eyes water as she watched Harlan's and Boyd's rapid approach.

"Okay. One at a time, folks," the sheriff said. "What's going on?"

"It's like this," Mitch began.

Jill stood by his side and mostly just listened until he was through explaining. She could tell that his injury was making him wobbly so she slipped her arm around his waist. "I think I hear the ambulance pulling up out front. Can I take him to get bandaged, Sheriff?"

"Fine. We'll finish up later."

When Mitch didn't argue, Jill figured he was hurt worse than he'd let on so she held tight and walked him out.

"You won't need a gurney," Mitch told the medics

when they threw open the rear doors of the ambulance and started grabbing supplies. "We're bringing the patient to you."

He plopped onto the rear deck and gave Jill a wan smile while the attendants helped him off with his jacket. "You'd better go back inside in case Harlan needs you. I'm in good hands."

"But…"

"Do it for Megan," Mitch said. "I'm not going anywhere."

"Okay." What she wanted to do was throw herself at him, rain kisses on his face and tell him that her heart had almost stopped when she'd realized he'd been wounded. But Mitch was right. They had one more loose end to tie up. The most important one.

Back inside, Jill continued to badger the sheriff. "You have to do something. Before they smuggle Megan out of the country."

"Take it easy. We're already working on that."

Jill thought he sounded like a grandfatherly figure trying to placate a flighty, overexcited adolescent. Well, she might be keyed up but she was far from childish, and nobody, not even Harlan Allgood, was going to get away with talking down to her.

"How? Where? When?" She glanced at the chair where the cops had secured Natalie. "She said Megan was being put on a plane in a couple of hours!"

"Not anymore she isn't," Harlan replied. "If you hadn't been running all over tarnation and getting yourself into trouble you'd already know that. The crooks we picked up for gambling were involved up to their necks in the kidnapping and the Pearson bombing. One of them decided to cut a deal and told us everything."

"Megan's safe?"

"Yes. She never left Fulton County. Adelaide is picking her up and bringing her in."

Jill was almost overcome with joy. She clapped her hands and grinned. "Praise the Lord."

"My sentiments exactly," the sheriff told her.

"I have to go tell Mitch!"

"Then go, before you bust a puckering string," Harlan teased. "Just keep me posted if they decide to send him to the hospital."

"Will do." Jill was already racing back toward the open door.

Mitch was still seated on the rear deck of the ambulance when she burst out of the factory. She began to shout, "They found Megan! She's okay."

There were tears in her eyes, and his, when she reached him.

"They rescued her? You're sure?"

"Positive." Jill's voice broke. Mitch had his shirt off and there was a white bandage taped over his ribs on one side. The realization that mere inches had separated the bullet's path from his heart made her stomach clench. Every nerve in her body fired repeatedly, sending shivers up and down her spine and tickling the hair at her nape.

She absolutely had to touch his arm as she explained, "Harlan sent Adelaide to pick her up."

"Thank God." Mitch placed his hand over Jill's where it lay on his forearm.

"How's it going for you?" she asked, eyeing his bandages and feeling her stomach knot in empathy.

One of the medics spoke up instead. "See if you can talk him into going to the hospital, will you? We'd like an X-ray of that wound to make sure there's no bullet fragments left inside."

"Later. I'm fine for now," Mitch said, trying to slip an arm back into his jacket sleeve and grimacing with pain at the movement. "I need to talk to Harlan. I intend to see Megan as soon as she's brought in."

Jill noted perspiration dotting his forehead and reached to help him dress. Instead of grabbing the jacket fabric, however, her hand somehow strayed to his cheek. She caressed it. Looked deeply into his eyes. Saw what she hoped was the same depth of emotion she herself was experiencing.

He covered her hand with his, then turned and placed a kiss in her palm. There was telltale moisture in his gaze. "I was afraid I'd lost you," he said softly.

"Never."

It was no longer necessary for Mitch to hold her hand. She wouldn't have moved away for anything. Instead, she slipped one arm around his neck, pivoted to face him, then lowered her other hand to his shoulder. The touch was gentle, as she'd intended, yet it was also meant to convey the love she could no longer hide or hope to deny.

"Is that a promise?" Mitch asked in a near whisper.

Jill nodded. "It's a lot more than that. I thought it was too scary to fall in love with a fireman because of the dangers you face all the time, but I guess I did it anyway."

"Did you? Are you sure about that?"

"Oh, yes. I'm positive." Blushing warmed her cheeks far more than the afternoon sunshine. To her relief and delight, Mitch began to smile, giving her the courage to ask, "Do you…? I mean, are you…?"

He started to laugh, then stopped short and pressed his arm against his side. "Ouch. Yes, honey, I love you, too. I have for a long, long time."

"Why didn't you *say* something?"

"Lots of reasons," Mitch told her. "I suppose I was worried that we might mistake friendship for something more and maybe lose the closeness we'd developed if we were wrong."

She stepped nearer, rested her forehead against his temple and closed her eyes. "I have never had a dearer friend than you, Mitch Andrews. I can't think of anyone I'd rather spend the rest of my life with."

"Are you proposing marriage?" he asked.

"I might be."

"Just so there's no question, will you marry me, Jill?"

In the space of a heartbeat she answered, "Yes!"

"Good. Now that that's all settled, let's find out where they're taking Megan. I need to be there."

"*We* need to be there," Jill corrected. "And if I have enough time I'll swing by the school and pick up the boys, too."

"Of course." Mitch got to his feet and straightened with difficulty, favoring his side. "The whole family needs to welcome her home."

It didn't escape Jill's notice that Mitch had referred to them as a family. She viewed them that way, too, and had for some time. Later, after things settled down and they figured out what the future held, she intended to suggest that she and Mitch consider adopting all three orphans.

Yes, it was an outrageous dream, but at this point Jill was ready for anything. Mitch loved her. Megan was about to be returned. And the culprits responsible for the factory bombing and fire had confessed. Any details beyond that were of little importance. At least for now.

She took Mitch's arm and held tight, matching his stride as best she could. The grin on her face was so wide she was sure she looked silly. Well, so what? She didn't mind if the whole town laughed at her. She'd never been happier and she didn't care who knew it.

At her side, she felt Mitch falter and saw him grimace. The look on his face grew incredulous. Then, his eyes rolled back and he started to slump to the ground.

Jill had to use every ounce of her strength to keep him from going down hard. She looked back at the ambulance, intending to call for help, and saw that the medics were already running toward her.

They had a backboard under Mitch and were loading him into the ambulance in minutes. He hadn't regained consciousness but they'd assured her his vital signs were strong.

"I'm riding with him," she said flatly. "Don't even think of going without me."

"Yes, ma'am. You want to run in and tell Harlan what's happened? He should be informed."

Jill hesitated. She had already promised to do that. "Okay." One long, loving look at Mitch was her gift to herself before she said, "I'll be right back."

She was beginning to feel as if she'd been running a marathon after all the afternoon's activity. In the factory, out of the factory, then back in again. This seemed idiotic. Why didn't the guys on the ambulance just radio their status?

Struck by that reality, Jill whirled in time to see the

EMT unit pulling out of the parking lot with Mitch inside. They were ditching her!

She continued to Harlan, grabbed his arm and shook it to get his full attention. "I'm heading for the hospital."

"Now?"

"Yes. My car's out back."

"Mitch was transported?" he asked.

"Yes. I wanted to ride with him but…"

"Enough said," the sheriff replied. "There's no way I'm letting you get behind the wheel when you're this upset. Come on. I'll take you."

Boyd waved a small, rectangular object at his boss as he passed. "What about the flash drive Natalie had on her?"

"Bag it and bring her in. We'll go over this place from one end to the other later."

"Natalie had a flash drive?" Jill asked as soon as she'd climbed into the patrol car. "Was that what she was looking for?"

"Apparently. I suspect it proves she's the one who's guilty of embezzlement."

"Why did she have to shoot Mitch?" Jill was too frightened, too stunned, too worried about him to weep, but her spirits had sunk as low as they could get.

"Because she wasn't rowin' with both oars in the water. The woman's a sandwich short of a picnic." He flashed a smile. "Don't worry. Mitch'll be fine."

"I wish I could believe you."

"Never mind me. Believe God. He'll take care of you."

"Like He took care of Mitch?" Jill countered.

"Nope. Like He took care of that little girl we're

about to meet up with," Harlan drawled. "Adelaide reported her ETA while you were outside with the medics. She should be gettin' to the hospital about the same time the rest of us do."

Time? Panicky, Jill looked at her watch. "Oh, no. It's after two. I need to pick up the boys at school."

"I'll do that for you as soon as I drop you off."

"Thanks."

Jill's mind was spinning, her thoughts so disjointed she wondered if she was much more lucid than Natalie was at the moment. It would have been terrible if she'd forgotten to go get those kids on time.

Then again, since the culprits were under arrest it was probably safe again. At least she hoped so. Until Harlan had everybody locked up in jail and had explained his conclusions she couldn't truly relax.

They pulled onto the hospital grounds and Harlan sped directly to the emergency entrance.

Jill was out of his car and running toward the E.R. before he had time to take his seat belt off.

She reached the door only seconds after the medics pushed Mitch through on their gurney. To her delight he was now awake and talking.

"You ditched me," Jill said, hitting one of the men on the upper arm before she reached for Mitch's hand. "That was a terrible thing to do."

"Just protecting our patient," he answered as he gave her a sheepish look. "If we'd known how mad he'd be when he woke up without you, we'd have taken you along."

"You missed me?" she said, focusing her undivided attention on the man she loved. "That's good to hear."

"I'm sorry if I scared you," Mitch said. "I've never passed out before."

"Well, see that it doesn't happen again."

"Yes, ma'am."

Smiling through tears of relief, Jill continued to hold his hand. "As it turns out, we're in just the right place. Adelaide is bringing Megan here."

"What about the boys?"

"Harlan's gone to pick them up." She laughed lightly. "I hope the teachers don't refuse to release them. I was pretty adamant about it when I dropped them off this morning." Sighing, she bent over the stretcher and kissed Mitch's cheek. "So much has happened since this morning it seems like a week has passed instead of only one day."

"That's because you were having so much fun hanging out with me," he quipped. "I really know how to show a girl a good time."

"Yeah, well, let's make our dates a little less exciting from now on, shall we?"

"Awww."

Jill was about to tease him more when the double doors swung open and the female deputy entered. In her arms was the child none of them had believed they'd ever see again.

Megan's short, curly hair was mussed and she looked as if she'd just awakened from a nap. Jill had never seen a lovelier sight.

Although Jill held out open arms, Megan leaned toward Mitch and reached for him.

He didn't hesitate. "Just give her to me for a second," he said, sounding choked up. "It's hard to believe I'm not dreaming."

Megan chortled and began to bounce the moment her feet touched the edge of the gurney.

Jill rescued Mitch by lifting the little girl away. "You'll get to play with him soon," she promised. "And Tim and Paul are on their way."

The little girl's dark eyes twinkled. "Tim? Paw?"

"That's right," Jill said, once again so happy she was almost in tears. "We'll get you and Uncle Mitch checked over and then hopefully we can all go home together."

Beside her, Jill saw Mitch reach for the toddler's bare foot and give it a gentle squeeze before he said, "That sounds like the best idea I've heard today."

He laughed aloud and grabbed his side when Jill arched one eyebrow and stared so pointedly at him. "Okay, the second best," he said with an earsplitting grin. "Marrying you is the absolute best. Honest."

EPILOGUE

Thanks to his injury, Mitch was forced to take the next three weeks off work. He chose to spend them with Jill and the children, much to her delight. Tim was still acting as if he didn't trust any adult to care for his siblings but there were times, like now, when his unnecessary concern came in handy.

She and Mitch were able to meet with Harlan and talk openly about the Pearson case because Tim was busy in the living room, showing Megan and Paul how to use the new teaching video Mitch had bought them.

"More coffee, Sheriff?" Jill asked, holding up the carafe.

"No, thanks. I'm fine. I just stopped by to fill you in on the latest."

She came to stand behind Mitch and touched his shoulder. He covered her hand with his and left it there while they both listened.

"Natalie was the instigator. And the embezzler, just like we thought. She'd lost piles of money gambling and was doing everything she could to blame it on others."

"Like the men Rob fired, you mean?"

Harlan nodded. "Particularly one of them. She'd cooked the books to make it look as if Vernon Betts was so old and addled that he'd made a bunch of costly mistakes. Now that it's all been sorted out, Thad's given Vernon his job back and says he's the best worker he's ever had."

"Wonderful." Mitch closed his fingers around Jill's and smiled up at her. "The kids are doing well, too."

"Looks like you all are," Harlan said knowingly. "Are you interested in hearing more about who took Megan and where she was all that time?"

"It was the gamblers, right?" Jill said, glancing toward the doorway to make sure the children weren't eavesdropping.

"Yup. It all made sense once I got the details sorted out. The woman who was babysitting Megan had no idea we were turning the town upside down looking for her. She'd been hired by Natalie's crooked buddies to take care of the little girl for a few days. As soon as they got the forged papers they needed, they were planning to ship the baby out of the country just the way Natalie said."

Jill felt Mitch's shoulder quiver beneath her touch. She knew how he felt. The thought of that innocent little girl being sold like an animal was enough to unnerve the strongest person.

"Thank God we found out in time," Jill said.

"Yeah." Harlan nodded sagely. "I know a lot of folks claim there aren't any more real miracles these days but this sure felt like one. Too many odd things came together just right for me to believe it was an accident that we figured everything out before it was too late."

He drained his coffee cup and pushed away from the table. "Well, I guess that's about it. Any other questions?"

"Only a couple," Jill said. "What about the man who chased me through the forest?" She felt Mitch's fingers tighten over hers as she added, "I'd hate to think he's still out there."

"He's not. I convinced the gamblers that the DNA in the lost stocking cap matched one of their samples and they couldn't wait to confess and blame each other."

"You didn't really have a match?"

"Not yet. Those tests can take months, especially if there's no threat to life involved. Now we won't have to worry about it."

Mitch was shaking his head. "Okay, we know they were responsible for the bomb, too. But what about the second set of arson fires? Why did they set those?"

"They didn't," Harlan said, looking at Jill. "Remember a teenager you fostered about a year ago? His name was Gilbert."

She nodded, thoughtful. "Of course. He had an unhealthy fascination with fire. That was one of the reasons I finally had to give him up."

"Well, it turned out he was the one who snuck around and lit those little fires. He said he was jealous when he heard you'd taken in a couple of younger boys and he just wanted to make trouble."

"So, all the threat is gone?" Mitch asked.

"Yup. Serenity has returned to Serenity." The sheriff levered himself to his feet. "So, when are you two gettin' hitched?"

"News travels fast in this town," Jill said, grinning back at Mitch when he smiled at her. "I guess we shouldn't keep everybody wondering. We've talked to Brother Malloy and it looks like he'll be able to perform the ceremony before Thanksgiving. We're looking forward to spending the holiday here, together."

"The kids too?" Harlan asked.

Mitch answered, "Yes. We're already like a family. If things work out the way we hope, we'll be adopting them real soon."

A collective squeal came from the direction of the doorway. Tim, Paul and Megan had overheard.

Mitch held out one arm toward them while Jill crouched next to his chair and did the same.

As the children gathered around her and the man she loved and they shared a mutual embrace, she realized that her fondest dreams had come true.

There was nothing more to say. They were a family.

* * * * *

Dear Reader,

I spent many years working with elementary-school children. That's probably why, when it comes time to write about them, I usually create characters between four and eight years old. Those are the ages I think I understand—as much as any adult can. In those days I saw my job as a way to demonstrate the love of Christ in a secular atmosphere. Now I do it mostly in print.

This is the first book in my new miniseries, The Defenders, that features the work of CASA volunteers. These court-appointed special advocates represent children in regard to the legal system, appearing before any judge who is being asked to decide their fate. It's a thankless, unpaid position that must make all of heaven rejoice, especially when there is a happy ending.

I pray that your personal happy ending includes a commitment to Jesus Christ. Mine certainly does. I love to hear from my readers. The easiest way to reach me is by email, val@valeriehansen.com, or send a letter to P.O. Box 13, Glencoe, AR 72539. You can also see my other work at www.valeriehansen.com.

Blessings,

Valerie Hansen

Questions for Discussion

1. Have you ever known a real firefighter? Was he or she like Mitch Andrews? In what ways?

2. Do you think Jill was being foolish to go to the scene of the fire? Were the other bystanders wrong, as well, or is it common for tight-knit communities to gather like that in times of tragedy?

3. Did you notice how well the boys accept the loss of their parents? Have you ever had to break news like that to a child? How did they react? How did you?

4. Do you know anyone who is a foster parent? How can the authorities tell which families are both willing and capable?

5. Have you ever imagined that the Lord is answering your prayers one way, then later discovered you were all wrong? Please explain.

6. People who are strong willed can be difficult to deal with. What's the difference between Jill and Natalie? How are they the same? Different?

7. You may have noticed that I chose not to include the impressionable children in the funeral plans. Should they have attended? Why or why not?

8. After Megan disappears, Tim, the oldest Pearson child, is much harder to handle. Are you the eldest

in your family, and if so, do you feel responsible for the younger members?

9. What about Jill's farm and house dogs? Are they necessary? Do they help the children adjust? Have you ever confided in a pet?

10. Jill is the kind of heroine who insists on getting involved, even though Mitch tells her not to. Are you like that? Has it gotten you into trouble in the past?

11. Why does Jill get mad at Mitch when he tells her he's just doing his job, rather than say he is acting solely on her behalf? Is that fair? Is it typical that he doesn't understand her female reasoning? How?

12. Mitch says something that isn't true when he's trying to distract the killer. Should he have stuck to the truth and trusted God to bail them out? Why or why not?

13. Lots of times people think they're doing the right thing, then later realize it was wrong. Is that an insurmountable sin or is forgiveness waiting?

INSPIRATIONAL

Inspirational romances to warm your heart & soul.

Love Inspired®
SUSPENSE

TITLES AVAILABLE NEXT MONTH

Available November 8, 2011

PRIVATE EYE PROTECTOR
Heroes for Hire
Shirlee McCoy

PROOF OF LIFE
Laura Scott

CHRISTMAS HAVEN
Hope White

BOUNTY HUNTER GUARDIAN
Diane Burke

LISCNM1011

REQUEST YOUR FREE BOOKS!

2 FREE RIVETING INSPIRATIONAL NOVELS
PLUS 2 FREE MYSTERY GIFTS

Love Inspired®
SUSPENSE

Love Inspired

Rodeo rider Wade Stone never thought he'd step foot in Dry Creek, Montana, again. But nine years later, he's back on Stone ranch, getting stared down by the townspeople. All *except* Amy Mitchell, whose heart he broke. With everyone against them, surely there's no second chance for this couple….

Sleigh Bells for Dry Creek
by Janet Tronstad

Return to DRY CREEK

Available November 2011 wherever books are sold.

www.LoveInspiredBooks.com

LI87703